NO MAN'S LAND

JACQUELINE DRUGA

VULPINE
PRESS

No Man's Land by Jacqueline Druga

Copyright © 2017 Jacqueline Druga

Published by Vulpine Press in the United Kingdom 2017

ISBN: 978-1-910780-68-8
Cover by Claire Wood

www.vulpine-press.com

ACKNOWLEDGEMENTS

I would like to sincerely thank those who walked this book along with me: Thank you to Paula Gibson who is always one text away. To Vulpine Press and Sarah Hembrow. Last but never least, my exceptional beta readers of my Apocalypse Facebook Group. They are the backbone of my process.

1

CHANCE

September 2

It wasn't supposed to happen like this.

We had been prepared, ready. We had done everything right.

It was supposed to be a happy day, not one filled with fear and worry. It was supposed to take place in a bright sterile room in a medically stellar facility, not a dark, vile and dilapidated tool shed in a stranger's backyard.

I envisioned my wife, lying in a clean bed, monitors strapped to her tight and large abdomen, the watery, swishy sound of a fetal heartbeat ringing loud in the room. Instead I watched her fight a birthing position, holding on to her stomach, while screaming to me, "Make it stop, Calvin, make it stop!"

The happy blessed event was to be witnessed not by nurses and doctors, but by mine and Leah's family who impatiently waited in a room, not far away, for the arrival of their first grandchild.

We were supposed to be surrounded by those we trusted and loved. Instead we were surrounded by the dead.

While they had many names, the Infected, the Formers, Virally Exposed or VEs, as Officials named them, most of the time I called them what they were... dead.

I felt utterly helpless. We sought shelter in the large tool shed because it was our only viable option. It was dank and smelled of rotten flesh. After I secured the door and pulled out the flash light, I realized the smell came from the bodies stored inside the shed.

They were placed there for a reason, perhaps a proper burial later. All of them had fatal head wounds, which told me they were sick at one point and had to be put down.

They weren't in any particular order, more like scattered about.

When we first took refuge in the shed, we were at a safe distance from the throes of dead that took over the area. Our light along with Leah's cries of pain attracted them faster, and they were relentless about trying to get in.

They caught the scent of life; it was their meal and they wanted it badly.

I wanted to tell her to stop yelling. To be quiet and maybe they would go away. I couldn't bring myself to be so heartless to her pain. I just had to focus on doing what I could, which at that moment was moving the bodies and trying to create a clean area for the arrival of our child.

"Calvin, this can't happen. We can't let this happen here," she cried.

"We don't have a choice," I said. "It is happening."

There was no doubt about it. Her waters had broken two hours earlier. We tried to keep going as long as we could. We moved slowly and steadily, leaving what would be considered a proverbial bread crumb trail of amniotic fluid.

Boards were missing from the side of the shed. Not many, but enough for the dead to reach through, trying to get us. It wouldn't be long before they ripped the place apart.

Leah wasn't well, I could see that. She hadn't eaten in two days and she barely took any water. I hadn't determined whether the birth of the child was a blessing, or a curse.

Whatever we viewed the birth, the truth remained: Leah wouldn't be around much longer.

She had been bitten.

The infection itself wasn't an overnight event, it was circulating around in her veins for a while. When it finally broke all boundaries, and turned the corner from being contained to out of control, the final part happened quickly. It seemed overnight. Up until then, authorities constantly fed us information, which kept us knowledgeable. We were relieved to learn the human being safest from the virus was the third trimester child still in the womb. They had already developed enough and even if the mother were to become infected, as long as the child was born before the mother died, the baby would be safe. They found that many newly born babies carried immunities.

There were so many reports of infants being born healthy and alive from an infected mother.

So there was a future generation who could survive the outbreak, if there was anyone left to care for the children.

The noise around us grew louder, arms and hands extended in.

"Stay away from the walls," I told her.

"They're gonna get in."

"Not if we're careful and quiet." I finished clearing a space in the center of the shed. "Sit down."

"Kill us." She pulled out the long kitchen knife from the backpack. One of several 'grab what could be a weapon' in a rush to leave our home. "Please. Kill us both right now."

She extended the knife to me and I took it. I would be lying if I said in that split second, I didn't think about doing it.

Leah was going to die anyhow. All that it would take would be to kill her and the baby would die along with her.

I couldn't. I took the knife, placed it behind my back and told her, "Don't be ridiculous. Now sit down."

As she lowered, a pain hit her. One that made her cradle her own abdomen, and drop to her knees.

Hurriedly, I crouched down before her. "What can I do?"

"Nothing," she grunted loudly, then released a long cry out. On all fours, she lowered her head. Leah's long hair dangled, covering her face.

"Maybe you need to lie down," I suggested. "Let me try to help you."

She screamed again, causing the dead outside to increase their pursuit in intensity.

"Leah, please, shh. You have to be quiet. They'll come crashing through."

"Maybe it's for the best."

Easy for her to say. I looked down to her arm, the one that had been bitten. The wound was still gaping open three days later. It failed to heal, in fact her arm had become discolored. She was more than likely in her latent state; she had developed what was called "the scent." Those about to succumb to the infection had an undetectable smell. They were hidden to the dead. I still was noticeable and so was our unborn child.

If the dead made it in, they would ignore her and rip me to shreds, then if our child was born, he would be taken too.

No. I couldn't have that. I wasn't ready to give up the fight.

"Stop. You have to stop. I know this is hard. I know this is painful," I said. "But please, try, for my sake, for our baby's, please, try to be quiet. We have a chance, Leah." I spoke soft. "We have a chance. They'll eventually go away. You have to stay quiet to give us that chance.

After a single whimper, she nodded then lifted her head. "I can't hold back. It's time," she said with quiet, breath-filled words. Her face was pale and her dark eyes locked into mine. "He's coming."

RECALL

93 Days Earlier

June 1

"He's coming."

Magdalene never knew the meaning of whispering. She hadn't a clue how to lower her voice. I attributed that to years of smoking and when she did talk softly, she squeaked. "He's coming," she whispered loudly again, peeking out the blinds of the back conference room.

I cringed.

"Yeah, well, he probably heard you, so there goes the surprise," I said.

She hushed me and waved her hand at me. She was a senior clerk at Bigby, Long and Thomas Accounting, the only other person there that could rival me for time with the company. Well, other than Martin Long.

He had been there the longest, outliving Bigby and Thomas and while nowhere near death, he was ready to retire.

Hence, the reason we all gathered in the big conference room.

Martin was on his last day, he was retiring. I don't think he expected a party, not on a Friday, when it was the norm to close shop early. Probably what Martin thought when he returned from a meeting.

I pitched in and awaited the 'late lunch, see ya, good luck' event.

The plan was for Martin's secretary to rush for him when he stepped from the elevator.

She did that.

She was to inform him he had an important meeting with a client in the meeting room. Obviously, she did that since he made his way to us.

Magdalene backed up, repeated her 'hush' and waited like a giggling school girl.

The door opened and we all shouted "Surprise!" as the light came on.

Martin did look surprised and somewhat embarrassed when we sang "For He's a Jolly Good Fellow."

He was a good sport, waving it off with a shy, "You shouldn't have." Then the party commenced.

After it calmed down some, people segregated into smaller groups. I sought some time with Martin and gave him my gift a bottle of scotch aged twenty years. Surprising me, he opened it and offered me a glass. I would have thought something that treasurable would be saved for a special occasion. I guess the party meant a lot to him.

"Oh, I shouldn't," I said.

"Come on, Calvin, I know you take the train." He showed me the glass.

It was a hefty helping, and I took it. After my first sip, I thought, *My God, this is good.*

"More?" Martin asked.

"I'm still working. So…" I set down my drink. "When do you leave for your Jules Verne?"

I asked about the 'Jules Verne' because that was the name Martin had given his retirement trip. It was in reference to *Around the World in Eighty Days.* He was going to see the world, literally, every country he could. In all the years he had worked and owned the company, the furthest away he had travelled was Atlantic City.

"Nope. Cancelled that. Margaret and I are going to Montana."

"Oh, wow, that uh sounds nice." I grabbed my glass. "For how long?"

"Indefinitely. Forever." He shrugged. "Four square miles, secluded land, mountain range gives natural protection to the east, a lake to the north. Very secluded. Easy to barricade. About right now…" He looked down his watch. "The trucks with the booze are arriving."

"Booze?"

"An astronomical amount. I have no plans to leave. Not for a while. I'll probably die there. If I leave and someone sees me, it's over."

"Martin," I chuckled his name. "What on earth are you talking about? Why Montana?"

"I just told you …"

"Yeah, yeah, I heard you."

"Calvin, don't you watch the news?"

"Oh my God, for real? You're worried about that?" I shook my head. "This has been going on for a year now. It's slowing down. Okay, I can see not leaving the country, but why go into hiding?"

"Not hiding, it's survival."

"It's over there."

"No, Calvin, it's here. It's been here for about two months."

I scoffed. I found that hard to believe. I really did. I followed the news. I knew what the virus was. It wasn't a virus. It was a weapon. A new one, hard to detect and the terrorists were dropping it left and right.

It would hit an area, everyone passed out and when they woke, they were like mad dogs. Some said they rose from the dead but there wasn't any proof of that.

"Who was best man at my wedding?" Martin asked. "I've bragged many times."

"General Sterling."

"Yes. He wasn't a general then. Is now. He's really big with the government. He says this thing is not a chemical weapon."

"It is."

"No, it spreads. It's airborne. Chemical weapons don't spread from person to person."

"Okay so it's a biological weapon," I said.

"That is now everywhere."

"Is that even possible?"

Martin nodded. "Do you know what North Korea did early on and everyone called them insane?"

"That's a pretty open ended question."

Martin smiled. "Funny. They created bunker cities. Prepared safe zones. One bunker city per region. When the region hit a percentage infected, the healthy were given the location of the bunker city and a certain amount of days to get there. After that, the region was cleaned."

"Why are we talking about North Korea?"

"Because we are doing the same thing."

I scoffed. "Marty, that's nuts. I haven't heard—"

"Why would you?" He cut me off. "Anyhow." He sat on the edge of the table. "I decided to make my own. My own safe place."

"In case the world ends?"

"Calvin, this virus is bad. It's coming in waves. Give it another month and warnings will be posted. One more month, it will be a daily battle. After then you'll be looking for news of Bunker cities. While me… I'll be watching a big wide open sky."

"You really believe that?"

"Calvin, the outbreak started in North Korea. The short destructive war between North and South. wasn't a war, it was self destruction for preservation."

"Why are you telling me this?"

Martin lifted his eyes and scanned the room. "I like these people, I do. You… I have known you since you clerked here at eighteen. How old are you now? Forty-five."

I cleared my throat. "Thirty-four."

"Jesus, we must be bad for you. Fact remains, I want you to know. I want… you and Leah to come to Montana. Come out before the baby is born. Be settled. I discussed this with Margaret we have invited a select few. We want you there. You'll have to drive out. It'll be a three day drive."

"When?"

"I think if you're diligent, you'll know when," Martin said. "Bob Scott and his family are coming out. We'll all be in touch. Just be there before the baby comes. Last thing you want is to have your wife give birth in a bunker city, or worse… in the middle of hell. Which this city will be if the virus takes over."

I wanted to laugh, but I didn't. I respected Martin and he was taking the outbreak, or whatever it was being called, very seriously. I listened to the news, I read articles, I was just as certain that it would pass. After thanking him for the offer, I told him, "We will be there if things go bad."

I meant what I said, even if I didn't believe it. After all, humanity was diligent, we would beat whatever it was, we always did, without a need to run to the hills, without a need to fear that my child would be born "in the middle of hell." Because I would never allow my son's birth to happen under those circumstances.

2

PUSH

September 2

It was hard to fathom how I could ever be irritated by the fact my wife was giving birth. I thought she was brave, yet, she folded. Okay, I get it, the pain was unbearable. Still, why didn't her maternal instincts kick in? Protect the child, or did she lose that because she herself was close to death? Maybe she wanted to take the baby with her.

Not me. For that moment, I worried about the safety of me and the baby. I knew, if we were just quiet, if there was no noise, the dead would move on. Sure they could sense us, smell us, but those weren't as strong of an attractor as noise.

With every wave of contraction came another scream, until, she started to wear down. I saw it, and heard it in her voice. Her face grew paler. Instead of on her back, legs spread wide, Leah assumed a squatting positions, held tight to her legs and shook her head.

"I can't. It won't come out."

"Yes. Yes you can." I moved closer to her, trying to encourage, trying to hide my concern and anger. "Come on, Leah push. Now!"

She grabbed tighter to her legs and grunted. One long, strong push and I saw the baby's head.

"It's here. I see the baby."

Another push and the entire head emerged. The baby was turning, eyes closed. I didn't know if he or she were dead or alive. Reaching out, I cupped my hand under the head and, bracing the neck with my fingers, I gently pulled.

A splash of blood emerged just after the baby. It was a boy and half his body was in my hand, and his legs hit the ground. Leah collapsed to her side in exhaustion, making it difficult to maneuver the baby.

He kicked, his mouth opened; he was perfect.

He was hard to grip, his body covered in a cheesy-like substance.

"We have a son, Leah." I smiled, then the smile dropped.

Leah wasn't moving, not at all. I glanced down to the baby in my hands, the cord ran from his abdomen to her vagina.

"Leah," I called to her. "Leah."

She didn't stir, in fact I couldn't even see her breathing. That was when it hit me.

What was I going to do? I never looked beyond the moment of birth. I never thought what I was going to do.

As Martin once said, "The world was hell, and I just allowed a baby to be born into it." What was wrong with me? What chance did my child have? The road ahead of us was long, my odds of survival were slim and his were even smaller.

As I grabbed the small scissors to cut the cord, I looked down at him and really contemplated my decision. It would be easy to accomplish, simply wrap the cord around his neck, place him next to Leah and let them both go.

The second I grabbed the cord to do so, I couldn't. It was my child. It was my job to protect him, to keep him safe, and to get him to a better place than a run-down shed.

I would. With that thought, I severed the cord and the baby from his mother.

Guilt consumed me for even thinking about it. I would mourn Leah and deal with her later, but first I had to care for my son. That was my priority.

Recall

45 Days Earlier

July 19

Martin was right. More than I wanted to believe, he called what was going to happen. I wanted to take Leah and leave, head to Montana, but within one month of Martin's retirement party, things were totally different.

Had we decided to leave just two days earlier, when Martin called and said, "Leave," we would have been close. At least out of city limits. Airline travel was cancelled, trains stopped moving, and busses only travelled within certain limits.

Major cities had been closed. Military moved in to keep law and order, and no one, absolutely no one, was permitted to leave. The only vehicles allowed in and out of the zones were delivery trucks and supplies.

There were ways around the barricade and people took them. Delivery trucks were one way and people bought passage.

Realistically, there was no way to barricade an entire city, unless of course it was Manhattan. I was fortunate not to be there.

Close enough though, I was in Philadelphia. A small borough inside the city limits. All highways were closed down and a curfew was in effect at sundown.

We were encouraged to go about our lives as normal as possible, and we tried.

I watched the news a lot, as did most people. America's version of bunker cities were less rumor and more fact. Pictures popped up daily on the internet. Large internment-style camps set up in the desert with high fences and huge water tanks. They were named Sanctuary Cities, each given a number.

The government vehemently denied them, stating they weren't needed. They swore the outbreak would be contained, or cured.

I spoke and communicated with Martin frequently. He kept telling me to leave. That soon enough, the sporadic infected would become hoards.

"Find an underground way," Martin said. "You have maybe a week or two tops, before those are shut down. Once you are out of the major cities, getting a car will be easy and just avoid highways. You need to go soon."

"What if we can't?" I asked.

"Then you're going to be trapped. It will get worse. You're Region Three. You're not getting out until they tap that region a dead zone and order evacuation for the Sanctuary City. Get out now before you can't move on the streets."

"We haven't been hit yet."

"You will. All populated areas eventually were hit."

By that, he meant hit with the virus.

No one could really pinpoint how the infection spread. It was a given it spread person to person, saliva, blood, bite, scratch, sex. However, the scariest part was that it was airborne. It seemed to move in waves. Hitting an entire area at once. Like parasites carried in the wind. Ninety percent of the area would become infected instantly. More than likely that was the reason everyone believed at first it was a weapon dispensed.

It was no weapon. It was a freak of nature. An extinction event. Labeled outbreak storms, the virus cloud, or whatever it was, would hit an area and then without warning, days later, maybe weeks, it would hit again. They weren't really storms, no thunder and lightning happened, no tornado or dark cloud rolled by. Everyone just dropped. A storm was about the best analogy given and it stuck.

Everything was given a name for ease.

The infected garnished the name "Vees" by everyone who talked about them. They were everywhere. It was frightening at first but then it became commonplace. News alerts would tell of areas to avoid because of Vee infestation and areas that were hit by outbreak storms.

Like war levels, there were Vee levels for an area. If one was spotted, the entire area was flagged.

We were fortunate, we hadn't actually seen one or watched a person die of infection. Other than on the news or the internet.

CBS ran a special on what to do if you or a loved one was infected with the Vee virus. Hotline numbers were in place to call and report a Vee, and the curfew was in place to get them all.

One would think a world besieged by plague and in a military state would be a chaotic one. People knew it was us against them. At least for the time being we were fighting together to live.

They were different than the stereotypical 'zombie' depicted in movies. Some moved slow, some fast. Never any superhuman feats of strength. The Vee were more reflective of how they were in life. Some only attacked for food when hungry, some just plain attacked.

I was working late, one of nine employees that remained in the company. Well, late by new standards. The city had hired any one that could to help run things. Our accounting firm handled the distribution inventory, and my bonus pay was rations.

There was no stopping at the grocer on the way home. Everything was distributed and accounted for. I had my day that I went to the store. Everyone did. The days of freedom shopping were gone. Even though we were told to go about our lives, things were changing and fast.

The curfew went into effect at seven in the evening. All internet services were blocked at that time and the only thing on television was the news.

Thankfully, I had saved all those DVDs

Finishing the day, I heard the alert of my phone. Figuring it was Leah asking what train I was taking, I lifted it. To my surprise, it was an alert from my bank, I was overdrawn.

I didn't know how that could be? I hadn't used the account in days, not since distribution.

Quickly, I went online and to my bank. The electric company payment cleared causing a deficit. It appeared earlier in the day, a huge withdraw had been taken out of the branch. Almost every dime we had.

I wanted to call the bank, but they closed at three. I sat there wanting to pull out my hair. Money wasn't important at that moment, but once the virus situation cleared up, it would be needed again.

My cell phone rang, nearly causing me to jump from my skin.

"Cal?" Leah called my name. "What train are you taking?"

A nervous twitch hit me, how was I going to tell her someone wiped out our account? "The uh, five ten."

"Can you catch the four thirty?"

"No, I have to finish up here."

"I need you to leave work early, Cal," she said calmly. "I have us a way out."

"What are you talking about?"

"The Save a Lot truck. I bought us passage. It cost—"

"Leah," I cut her off. "Did you drain the account today?"

"I did. It was the only way to get us out. We need to be at the warehouse by six thirty. We'll wait in the truck until it's ready to pull out."

"We can't do that, Leah. It's illegal."

"Too bad. We need to get to Montana. The truck will take us as far as Beaver County. My father will meet us there. We'll head to Montana. We need to get to Martin's place."

"Yeah, well, we should have gone when we had the chance. You didn't want to."

"I want to now. Be home, Calvin. I love you, but I will go without you. This baby is my top priority."

Then she hung up.

What was she thinking? Our suburb was safe, we were far enough out of the city and there had been zero reports of Vee in our area. Plus, our home was secure. Our house was on a small hill with a long set of stairs leading to the front door. The porch was easily blocked, and our first floor windows weren't ground level. So even if Vee made it up the hillside, they couldn't break through the windows. We had supplies. The news hadn't spoke of Sanctuary City retreats. Leaving was a mistake, I believed it.

However, I had to go where she went. Leah and the baby were my family. I hurriedly finished my work, and made it with a minute to spare, catching the four-thirty train.

There was a strange and different feel to everything when I left work. It felt like a holiday, like the time I went to work on Thanksgiving. No one was around, no one on the streets.

There were three other people on the train; they all got off before me.

My stop was the last one, and when I disembarked, I saw the parking lot. It was empty. My car was the only one remaining.

Had I missed something? Admittedly, I was so busy at work, I never listened to the news or checked it. Surely, Leah would have told me if something happened. I had my phone set up to receive Vee alerts. Nothing came through.

There was a scary sensation around me, a deadness to the air, it just didn't feel right. When I reached for the handle, I paused when the sound of air raid sirens blasted through the air. It wasn't the first time I'd heard them. They were commonplace because they were a means to call upon the volunteer fireman in the area when there was a fire.

These sounded different. Perhaps it was my imagination, but I felt they were different. I hurriedly got in my car and pulled from the lot.

Instantly, I turned on the radio The Emergency Alert System was playing mid-cycle.

"…urging citizens to remain in their homes and vigilant…" The robotic female voice said.

I kept changing the station hoping to catch it, but it was the same message, played at the same time on all stations.

Finally, it repeated.

"This is the emergency alert system. This is not a test. Citizens of the greater Philadelphia and surrounding areas be advised. The area is under a level three warning…"

Level three. That was the highest it could be. Usually we weren't under even a level one. Never a level three. That meant that one of those waves of outbreaks finally hit our region. How many people were struck? Was it wide spread or sporadic?

The automated message didn't give that information.

"Immediate infection outbreaks have been confirmed in the following areas ..."

The streets and areas were read off like a computer reading text to speech. As soon as I heard Powell Street in Springfield, I knew it was too close to home.

The short two-mile drive to my house was an adventure, more like a video game. There was a mad rush to leave; cars were driving erratically and fast. Pulling out without stopping, running red lights. It was stop and go for me, dart and move. Holding my breath, hoping some car didn't fly out from a side street and T-bone me.

To go where? Another area? The current retreat and safety place was Springfield Mall. Were they all going there? Surely, they weren't getting on the highway, it was blocked off, as were many of the main roads. Then again, I knew getting out of the city and area wasn't an impossibility. There were side roads and lesser-known routes.

Authorities advised people not to take those roads. They were jammed tight with vehicles and people ended up getting stuck when they ran out of gas. There were countless stories online. The worst happened outside of Boston. Citizens tried to escape, traffic came to a standstill and all it took was a few Vee and the gridlock quickly turned into an all they could eat buffet.

I made it to my street, a small dead end road, where one side was the 'flat' side where the homes set flush with the road, the other the 'high' side where the homes were on a hill. Cars where whipping out of the driveways, backing up and speeding away.

As soon as I pulled to the curb, I saw my neighbor loading his car.

"You better get moving, Calvin," my neighbor, Bill, yelled. "You don't have much time."

I raced around my car and to Bill. "What's going on? I didn't hear anything. I was on the train."

"Outbreak storm hit all over. They say for a fact it hit the entire area north of Powell," Bill said. "Authorities can't get in there fast enough to get them all. So you know what that means. In about an hour, Vee will be everywhere. Get out now."

"And go where?" I asked.

"East, south, they said Swarthmore is setting up a secure area. Anywhere but here, Powell is four streets over, Cal. Get your wife and get out."

"Don't you think if we hunker down and wait until authorities clean up?"

Bill laughed at me as he secured a bungee cord to the roof of his SUV. 'If they don't. You're stuck here."

"Cal!" Leah called my name and I turned my head to see her on the porch.

"Get your wife and go," Bill said. "Now."

I nodded and rushed up the steps to my porch.

"I tried to call you. I couldn't get through," Leah said. "I'm trying to pack."

"No," I shook my head. "Just pack what we can in a backpack. The Save A Lot warehouse is only three miles south. Worse comes to worse, we can walk with a backpack for three miles."

"What about all of our stuff. We have so much."

"We lock it up," I said. "We need to. In case we have to come back."

"Will we?" she asked.

"You got us a ticket on that truck," I said. "Hopefully, we'll be out of here by nightfall."

We were out of the house in a few minutes. I swore it took longer for me to lock up than it did to pack the backpack. We didn't need much. We just had to get out of the quarantine zone.

The Save a Lot truck was parked just outside the loading docks. Several cars were parked behind the building and the rear end was open.

Leah had explained that for three days she was working on getting us passage in the truck. He would take ten people, hidden behind a phony wall of boxes.

I felt relieved when I saw it there, but unsettled because there was no one walking around.

"Let's just get in the truck," I said, shutting off the car. "Do we have a secret code, a pass, what?"

"I met with him this morning. He knows us."

We both opened our car doors at the same time and stepped out. I reached in, grabbed the backpack and tossed it over my shoulder.

"Cal, something is not right."

"I know."

Where was everyone? The truck driver? The passengers?

I wanted to call out, but I didn't. As we moved closer to the tractor trailer we saw the first body.

It was a man, a younger man. His lifeless body was contorted on the ground. His back arched with chest outward, his legs bent in different directions as if he fell from a huge building.

I knew the look; I saw it on the news enough. The white pasty skin with dark blotches. The bleeding from the eyes, nose, and mouth.

Holding out my arm, I stopped Leah. "Stay here. Get ready to run back to the car."

I nudged the man's body with my foot. He was hard. I walked closer to the back of the truck.

More bodies were in there.

"Shit." I spun around to Leah. "The Storm hit here. Who knows when and how long we have. We have to get out."

"The truck," Leah pointed. "It has permission to leave. Are the keys inside?"

It was a good idea. Take the truck and roll out. The only problem was, what to do with the ten or so bodies in the back. Take a chance and precious time to move them out?

Again, I told her to stay back near the car as I moved to the cab of the truck.

I wasn't short, but I wasn't a tall man and I couldn't see up inside the cab. I climbed on the side step and reached for the door.

Before I even opened it, a Vee suddenly appeared inside, snarling and biting the window. His hands smacked hard against the glass in his plight to get at me.

I stumbled and tripped in my shock, landing on my backside. I cringed in pain and rolled to my side.

"Leah," I called out. "Get in the..."

Leah screamed. I was instantly hit with energy to get to my wife. I rolled to a stand, grabbed the backpack and headed toward the scream.

I expected her to be by the car, after all that was where I told her to go. Yet, she was near the truck, backing up as the Vee headed her way.

"Run, Leah, to the car."

She was too scared to move, I could see it on her face. I barged forward, swinging the backpack, hitting the Vee as I did, until I made my way to her.

"Move!" I ordered, grabbing her arm and pulling her to the car.

She kept screaming, and her screams attracted more.

It wasn't just the ten or so who came from the truck, Vee came from behind the warehouse and across the lot.

None of them were those passive ones I had heard about.

I shoved her in the car and raced around to my side, just as four or five Vee hit our car. One threw himself on the hood and began banging his head and hands on the glass.

I had to hurry, there literally was no time. After starting the car, I put it in gear, jerked the wheel and hit the gas.

Hood ornament Vee flew off and I careened into another one sending her flying.

There had to be at least five that I hit. The bangs and thumps against the car as I connected and the jolt of the wheels, as if going over a speed bump, when I ran them down told me so.

We managed to get out of that lot. Leah was hysterical. Surprisingly, I remained calm.

"It's okay. We're fine." I grabbed her hand. "We're good."

I had been holding my breath and released it slowly. My heart raced out of control, but for the sake of my wife I had to appear confident and unshaken.

We made it from the lot but we weren't in the clear. Vee were in packs at every corner we turned. If we made a left, we had to back up or make another left.

It was as if we were in a maze, being led one place to another. That place was our home. We couldn't go forward, we had to go back. We didn't have a choice.

3

NAME

September 2

He was naked and prefect, probably cold and it broke my heart that I instantly loved him so much. I wanted not to. I didn't want to feel a connection to my son. Not in this world.

I grabbed one of Leah's shirt form the pack and after using the drinking water to clean him, I swaddled him tightly.

He'd need to eat soon. I was glad Leah and I came up with a contingency should he be born on the run, and Leah unable to feed him.

I'd break out that bottle soon enough, but he wasn't fussy or crying. He kept staring at me, trying to focus. I could tell. His little mouth opening and closing, as he produced the quietest of newborn whimpers.

I just wanted to hold him and stare right back. Believe for a moment that all was right in the world. It wasn't and I had another problem to face.

Leah.

She had been bitten and she had died. It was only a matter of time before she rose.

Leah was my wife for a decade; I loved her like no other and believed she was the heartbeat of my existence. Now, she was gone. I was angry because I couldn't even mourn her. Couldn't take time to break down and cry because I had to think about how to put her down.

She was still on her side, the lower half of her body naked and painted in blood. The umbilical cord extended from her and I could see the placenta partially expelled.

She died right after giving birth. Collapsed and died. I knew because not only wasn't there a sound, there was no more free flowing blood.

A part of me believed I needed to do something before she woke up. It seemed wrong and like a desecration. Almost as if a part of me was hoping she wouldn't wake up.

I didn't even know how I would accomplish it, what I would use. How would I do it with a baby in my arms? I couldn't put him down, what if she lunged and got him?

Whatever way I picked it wasn't going to be easy.

Since the outbreak in my town, I had run from many Vee. I fought off and distracted more than I could count. Yet, I killed only a handful. It wasn't for lack of trying, I did try.

Taking out the Vee wasn't easy. Not emotionally or physically. The only way to kill a Vee was to destroy the brain. It was harder than it sounded. At the point when a Vee just turned, they were still solid. The flesh hadn't rotted. Sharp objects didn't go easily through bone and breaking a skull is not a piece of cake. An ax or hatchet was ideal, but they were difficult to maneuver or swing. If you didn't get them the first time, your next delivery would lose strength.

I didn't have a gun, even I if did, the shot would attract more Vee. Experts claimed the best weapon was a knife. Use it through the eye or temple.

Again, another situation easier said than done. The knife wasn't ideal.

It plunges into the soft flesh with ease. It was creepy and caused me to get physically squeamish and shiver. Much like fingernails down a chalkboard. The movies had it all wrong. There was no aiming a gun at a loved one when you knew they were infected. You feel bad for a moment and then bang. It wasn't that easy. Anyone you knew was hard to take out. It was hard to see that they weren't anything more than sick human beings. Even a crazy neighbor, no one immediately went for the kill, it was instinctive to avoid them and run....

That was how it got out of control. No one wanted to kill someone they knew and loved.

I was no different.

I didn't want to kill Leah again. My choice was gone, I didn't have one.

She stirred some, then opened her eyes.

RECALL

3 DAYS EARLIER

August 31

There was a learning process, an educational window before the world shut down. Most people were too busy running trying to find a safe place, and they never paid attention.

We did.

After the insanity at the warehouse, we managed to make it home. There wasn't any rash movement of Vee, like Bill had said, the streets were pretty calm. We actually felt relatively safe, only a few times were there instances of Vee coming after us. It was during one of these times, I killed my first one.

He was on our porch, the only one to make it up. Fearful that he was going to get in, I grabbed a baseball bat and stepped out to confront him. It wasn't my slug of the bat that killed him. I ended up hitting his shoulder and he flew backwards down the steps, landing with a final crack of his skull on the concrete.

We had so much food, so many supplies. We contemplated staying.

For the first two weeks, the news played constantly. The fed us information and we learned it. The internet went down right away so the news was our source.

The Vee were their most violent when they were infected directly with the airborne virus. The virus caused the lungs to bleed, the bronchial tub to swell and the victim, unable to breathe drops where they are.

Within minutes they are dead.

An hour later... they rise.

The worst ones. Those who were bitten or infected via secondary route were more docile and didn't tend to attack on instinct, they only attacked for food.

They all had one thing in common... they were dead.

Just after the television went off, Leah and I went into great lengths discussing what we should do. We really wanted to stay, at least until the chaos subsided and the world went quiet. Getting away and out of the city would be easier.

Then came the drop.

We heard the plane first and were worried that it would attract Vees. When we looked out to see if any were coming, we watched sheets of paper rain down from the sky.

An old-fashioned method of getting the message out.

The flyers were our warning to leave.

It also was the first official confirmation of Sanctuary Cities. Ours was number sixteen and in Morehead, Kentucky. I immediately pulled out a map. It was located about fifty miles east of Lexington and I could see by the map why it was chosen. It was easy to seal off the highways in and out and it was nestled in the mountains.

That was well over six hundred miles to travel. Though it was closer than Montana. Even though my vehicle was more of a wagon than car, I got good mileage. I had enough fuel, confidently, to make it nearly three hundred miles. That was half way there. There were places listed as transportation hubs to the city. Dates to be there by. Perhaps I could get to one of those.

Our Sanctuary City was scheduled to shut its gate and take in no more survivors after September 30.

With nearly a month to get there, it was more than doable. We couldn't piss around though, because the flyer also warned our region was scheduled for Vee mass extermination two weeks before the gate shut down.

I knew what that meant. We had to get out.

There were a few cars remaining on the street, and I syphoned what I could from their gas tanks. I knew fuel would eventually be a problem. We packed our vehicle, I believed we were smart. We had enough time to think ahead, what we would need, down to the baby supplies. We grabbed one of those carriers that went over the back or chest, just in case we had to walk. We even stole the neighbor boy's red Radio Flyer wagon. Never did we take for granted that we wouldn't have to eventually move on foot.

That small hatched cargo area was jammed packed. With the exception of the fuel cans there was nothing we could carry and fit in that Radio Flyer.

The first day out went well and was pretty easy. Avoiding the highways, we took mostly back roads and made quite a bit of distance.

We saw a lot of Vee. As we drove by them they'd extend their arms like dead hitchhikers.

We didn't however see people.

None that were alive, anyway.

Had they all died, or were they tucked away safely in a sanctuary city? Admittedly, Leah and I were behind the eight ball. We stayed when others pulled out.

I thought for sure that somewhere around Interstate 68 we'd hit some free and clear roadway. From a distance it looked good, but when we actually drove the highway, we saw how bad things were.

One side of the highway was at a standstill. I stepped out to take a look at the sea of abandoned cars.

But they weren't really abandoned. The smell of rotting flesh filled the air and the humidity made it worse. Body parts strewn across the road. Partially eaten corpses were half out of their cars. Probably bitten and beaten down when they attempted to flee.

"What now?" Leah asked. "Turn around?"

I shielded my eyes from the sun and peered around. The other side of the highway didn't look quite as bad. That was the route we'd go.

Cautiously, so as not to cause damage, we drove across the wide open median, making it to the other side. From there we got a good thirty miles until we had to stop again.

I didn't worry, there were maybe ten cars.

After getting out of my own vehicle, I examined the scene. It wasn't a traffic jam, but an accident. A large white pick-up was on its side blocking half the road. Directly before it, cutting off any way to pass, was a little blue car.

The rest just created a chain reaction fender bender. It was more than that. The Vee had passed through. More carnage was on the road way, flies buzzed over the remains and I heard a slurping sound.

"Cal?" Leah called my name.

"Stay in the car," I told her.

"What are you doing?"

"I just need to move that blue car and we can get through."

"I'll help." She had stepped from our car and leaned against the hood.

"Leah, please. Get back in the car and shut the doors."

"Why?" She lifted her hands. "It's fine. No one's around."

I knew that wasn't the case, because that slurping sound continued. I walked slowly through the line of wrecked cars. We could get through, all I had to do was move that blue car. Then my foot hit something and I looked down. Immediately, I was sick to my stomach. It was bloody, tiny shoe. Just beyond it was a doll, a pink backpack and more 'child' items. I wondered if they had been in the one and only minivan on the road.

As I passed it, I saw the door was open and I promised myself I wouldn't look. That was until I realized that was where the slurping sound came from.

I paused only a second, looking side-eyed into the van.

Inside was a child, a boy of maybe eight. His hair was probably light, but it was hard to tell with the blood matted to some of it. His face was gray with purple spots and streaks of veins, his eyes translucent. He held in his hand some sort of organ and he gnawed and slurped it like corn on the cob. When he saw me, he lifted his eyes and snarled at me.

I kept on walking.

From what we heard on the news, an eating Vee was a safe Vee until they needed more food.

He was preoccupied and that blue car was right there.

I approached the car, listening for the slurping in case it stopped. The driver's door was open, there was no one inside and the key was in the ignition. After checking back to make sure van boy wasn't coming, I tried to start the car.

Nothing.

I moved the key in the 'on' position, shifted the gear to drive, and holding on to the frame of the driver's door, I pushed the car. It wasn't hard and once it moved, it moved directly to the side of the road, and the momentum of the slope took over and the car rolled down the grade.

"Yes," I said with a victorious smile. Then I realized the slurping had stopped.

I spun around quickly. Where was he? I didn't see him or hear him.

How stupid was I? I walked away from my car without a weapon or means of defense.

After grunting, "Shit," I assessed how far away from my car I was. Thirty feet maybe? I could run, get in and drive out of the situation.

Then I saw Leah get out again.

What was she doing?

Shaking my head I hurried her way, but half way there, I saw it before she did. A little girl Vee was to her left on the side of the road. The child wore a blood stained white tee shirt and purple shorts.

At that moment, I ran. "Get in the car! Now!" I shouted.

"Why?"

Why? Why would she even take a second to ask? I was running, I was screaming. Was she that much in denial? Before I even arrived, before I guess she could process my yelling, Vee Girl lunged at Leah and latched onto her arm. The force of the child knocked Leah a bit off her balance and into the side of the car.

She screamed and tried to pull the child from her.

As I ran, I watched the struggle and saw Van Boy. He ran my way, but wasn't fast enough. We crossed paths and I arrived at Leah.

She screamed at the top of her lungs, loud and shrill. I grabbed Vee Girl and whipped her small body as hard as I could from Leah. She pulled the flesh right from Leah's arm, and had it in her mouth. Blood poured out of my wife and I tossed the child. She didn't weigh much, and my adrenaline fueled my strength. Vee Girl landed with a 'thud' on the road.

I shoved a hysterical Leah in the car and raced around to my side.

Van Boy arrived.

Hurriedly, I got inside as the boy leapt on the hood of my car. I jolted the car in gear and slammed the gas causing him to roll off.

I couldn't move very fast, it was an obstacle course of vehicles. Carefully, I drove around the cars, looking in my mirror. The Vee children had collected themselves and were following. The little girl's leg dragged behind her.

Leah cried, and there was nothing I was able do at that moment to help her. I had to get free and clear and to the open side of the road. Once I did and we were safe, I'd pull over and see what I should do.

Bottom line was, she had been bitten and other than trying to stop the bleeding, there wasn't much more I *could* do.

4

CHOICE

September 2

I couldn't do it.

When Leah smoothly rolled from her side to a sitting position and looked at us, I cringed and froze. Then I thought, *You know what? This is it. This is how it ends.*

I prepared to die holding my newborn son because I just couldn't kill Leah. I had weapons, not a gun, but weapons: a huge wrench, a hammer, a bat. All of which were at my disposal, none of which I could bring myself to pick up against her.

How? How do I just simply bash in the brains of someone I loved?

I cradled the baby into my chest, lowered my head to his and waited.

Then it was easy. Leah wasn't violent. She didn't lunge at us. It was almost as if a part of her knew us and remembered us. Then she became preoccupied with the placenta that slipped from her body. She lifted it and slowly began to consume it.

We weren't on the menu at that moment. It gave me time to figure out what I was going to do.

Keeping her - for lack of a better word - alive, had its advantages. I always knew the Vee could hear and see us. I theorized they could smell or sense us. That theory was somewhat proven true when Leah reanimated. From that moment on, the viciously attacking Vee started to leave. The ones that reached in through the broken walls and tried to get us, tried no more. It could have been, as I predicated earlier, because we were quiet and Leah wasn't screaming. A part of me believed not only could they not hear us, they couldn't smell me and the baby, so they moved on.

That left one problem solved, the other was nightfall. We couldn't go anywhere until the sun came up. Simply because I couldn't see a foot in front of me at night.

That shed was only going to get darker. I wouldn't have worried about it so much, had it not been for Leah and worrying what she was going to do once she finished her placenta.

In the dark, my eyes wouldn't adjust. I wouldn't see her coming at all.

I had to chance it and use the small, round, battery operated closet light I had. It didn't give a lot of light, but enough for me to watch Leah.

I had to pick my battles. Take a chance of sitting in the dark or having the Vee outside see the light.

Without sound or scent, I was hoping the light didn't draw them in. Maybe they moved on. They did that. After failing at a food source, they eventually walked off.

I'd deal with them in the morning.

The car wasn't that far, but with the overcast sky and no moon I couldn't see it. I hoped at first light no Vee would be outside and I could make a quick escape.

As the hours passed the temperature dropped. All I could do was sit there shivering, holding the baby, hammer at my side, while I watched Leah and waited for her to attack.

5

CHASE

September 3

I gave my son a name. I called him Edward. The baby's name was always a source of contention between Leah and myself. She wanted to name the baby one of those names that no one ever pronounced correctly. I wanted to give the child something old-fashioned, like John or Jill. I thought ahead to their old age and what name would be fitting for a senior citizen.

Now it didn't matter. Chances were Edward would probably never see his first birthday. Not in this world.

The tiny circle light was enough and I kept my eye on Leah. When I realized she wasn't immediately attacking after her placenta meal, I pulled the duct tape from the bag, set the baby on my jacket and ripped a long piece. Carefully I approached her. She perched on her knees and moved her head my way, snapping her jaws in my direction, trying to bite me.

I was ready for her to lunge, but she never did and I took advantage of that. When I felt confident, I placed the strip of duct tape over her mouth.

She shook her head violently, trying to shuck the tape. While she did that, I bound her hands. Then after the initial taping, I reinforced.

I didn't know how much was left in her brain, but common sense was gone. Not once did she reach up her hands to her mouth.

After several minutes of thrashing and tossing herself around, Leah gave up. Almost in defeat she sat back down on the ground.

I suppose it was wrong to duct tape her. To let her suffer. But I just couldn't bring myself to kill my wife.

Dead, alive, infected, whatever... she was still my wife.

It would have been physically simple to grab the hammer, walk over and smash it down to her skull. No matter how she appeared, she was Leah.

Before becoming infected there was nothing bad I could ever say about her. She was kind and loving, unselfish to a fault. Leah was a first grade teacher who cared more about her students than she did anything else. She brought the joys and problems home and worried about students during break.

With all that kindness how could I do it? Even though the experts said she wasn't my wife, how did I know? What if she just couldn't control what she did? What if my Leah, my beautiful Leah, was inside that shell of a body crying out, "Calvin please help me. Help me, Calvin"?

I didn't sleep the whole night, which wasn't good. I had to care for the baby, protect him. If I was tired and weak then I wasn't any good to my son.

It had been three days since we left our home, at first making lots of miles, then Leah was bitten and we had to stop frequently. The infection didn't really seem to hit her at all, with the exception of the wound. It didn't want to heal. She showed no signs and I thought maybe she didn't get infected at all until she went into labor. That was when the fever started and Leah grew weak.

Her water had broken and giving birth on the road didn't seem like an option. We saw the lone house in the distance. The house ended up being filled with Vee and by the time we decided to run back to the car, we were surrounded. The only option was the shed.

Hours later, after Edward was born, the night was quiet and I just had to wait.

There was gas in the car, I had siphoned some, it would take us into West Virginia. Things were going to be harder with the baby. I'd have to stop often, stay away from crowds and find a secure spot, because eventually he was going to wail like babies often did.

I spent the night talking to Edward, telling him I would find him clothes and get him food. I promised him I would do everything I could to protect him. All while talking to him, I kept watching Leah.

Dawn arrived. I could feel the shift in temperature and smell it in the air. Bag over my shoulder, I swaddled the baby as best as I could and peeked out the open board of the shed.

A fog had set in; it wasn't thick, but enough to add a haze. I could see the car about a hundred feet away. The day before we pulled on to the property in a hurry, leaving the car in the front lawn. Holding the baby in my arms, I looked down to Leah.

"I have to go. I'm sorry. I will always love you." I closed my eyes tightly, then quietly opened the door.

I looked from right to left and didn't see any Vee. Baby in my arms, I hurriedly raced to the car and got there unnoticed.

The hoard of Vee had moved on, but they weren't far, I could smell them in the air.

Edward whined and whimpered a little and it sounded so loud. I opened the car door, tossed in the backpack and slid inside.

I had to keep him in my arms and drive that way. Once the fog lifted and it was easier to see, I would pull over and find that baby carrier. I would strap him to my chest as I drove.

"It's okay, it's okay," I told the baby, then pressed my lips to his head. "Shh." I inserted the key in the ignition and started the car. "It will be—"

Slam!

The sound of something suddenly hitting my window caused me to jump. I quickly put the car in drive and readied to slam on the gas, when I saw.

It was Leah. She was at my side of the car.

Her hands kept hitting the window, squeaking as her fingers slid down.

After mouthing, "I'm sorry," I slowly depressed the gas and pulled out. Carefully, I drove from the lawn to the driveway. I didn't want to gun it and take a chance of hitting or running over something, damaging our only means of transportation.

Once I pulled to the street, I sighed in relief. The road seemed free and clear. Then I looked in the rearview mirror. My heart sunk.

I saw Leah. Her arms, bound at the wrist extended as if reaching out. The sad part was, she wasn't just standing there, she was following us. Watching us go, staggering along, naked from the waist down from giving birth, trying her best to catch up, as if to say, "Don't leave me. Please, don't leave me."

I deliberately slowed down to see what she would do. Leah didn't give up. She fell twice, got back up and continued to try to get us. Even though I knew she was infected, that she was a Vee, it broke my heart to watch.

I couldn't go any further.

I stopped the car.

RECALL

7 MONTHS EARLIER

Leah rambled that day. In fact that was typical for her to do when she was nervous or anxious. Leah was on pins and needles. I didn't know how to ease her mind. I was divided between checking my emails on my phone and listening to her while we sat in the waiting room of the doctor's office.

"What if I'm not?" she asked.

"Then you're not."

"How can you be so insensitive?" she asked. She clutched her purse tight to her lap like a security blanket. Her legs tight together, her knees raised as her feet rested on the floor on her tip toes. I could feel the vibration next to me when she slightly bounced her legs.

"I'm not being insensitive," I said. "I'm not. Just... if you aren't pregnant nothing I say or do is going to change that fact this very second, will it?"

"So you don't think I am?"

I exhaled in frustration. "I didn't say that. You should have taken the test at home."

"No, what if it said I was and I wasn't."

"Oh my God." I rested my head back against the wall. "Leah, stop this."

"I want to be so bad."

"I know."

"I just can't lose another baby, Calvin. I can't."

That made me stop. I understood that because I didn't want to lose another one either. All the losses were early, but still losses nonetheless. The joy of finding out we were pregnant, then just before we'd hear the heartbeat, she'd miscarry. Three times it had happened and there was still no indication that anything was wrong. The doctors all said there was no reason she couldn't carry one to term.

There we sat again, waiting to see the doctor. It was the first time we didn't take one of the 'pee on a stick' tests. Leah suspected she was, but wanted to go to the doctor to be sure.

As odd as it sounded, all the anxiety that was with us that day, it was the last normal morning we would ever have. The last normal morning the world would have.

Things would forever change. The days of waking up to see the news about global conflicts, arguments about gun control, and people's rights ended that afternoon. All that gradually became obsolete.

We as a human race were about to embark on a different fight. A fight for our very existence.

I don't think when it happened, we pegged it as the day. But thinking back to that afternoon in the doctor's office, we witnessed the start.

"Why is it taking so long?" she asked. "I mean really."

"You're impatient."

A nap. I thought maybe if I closed my eyes, time would move faster and I'd be able to block out her constant neurotic talking. I was nervous, too. Wasn't she even concerned about that?

Just as I closed my eyes, I heard the female voice ask, "Do you mind?"

I looked and the office nurse was standing there with a remote. She turned off the 'I love Lucy' reruns.

"I have to see," she said and changed the channel to the news.

I sat up. Looked at the screen. A breaking news ribbon ran across the bottom, 'Riot's in Atlanta.'

"What's going on?" Leah asked.

"I don't know," the nurse said. "It started with a few people attacking each other."

"Drugs," I said. "Must be drugs. Something new. You watch."

"I don't know." The nurse shook her head. "They say they aren't even stopping for the police."

"Look at all that blood," Leah commented. "What is this world coming to?"

It was rhetorical question, I suppose. I mean, how many times had I heard it said in my life?

Watch a fight...

What is this world coming to?

A war breaks out.

What is this world coming to?

Leah didn't expect an answer, probably because she didn't think there was one. But unknown to us in that room, that day there was finally an answer to that question.

What is this world coming to?

Its end.

6

COMMITTED

Edward cried only a little bit. I feared his tiny lungs weren't developed enough. That was something we learned in prenatal classes. He needed to cry, to scream to push his lung capacity. I felt horrible allowing him to fuss and cry, but there were no doctors, he had to be strong.

That was a must.

It was funny looking back to those classes. I imagined years or even months earlier those classes were different. Before the virus the classes probably taught how to prepare for birth, when to go to the hospital, how to recognize danger signs. All those things including nursing and post birth care.

It changed when we started classes after the outbreak. Sure it included all those things, but by government standards they had to include how to deliver a baby outside a hospital, and how to cut the cord and deal with the placenta. Although Leah handled that portion on her own.

In class we learned how to keep the baby warm, how to be proactive about feeding the child should the mother die, and how to humanely take the baby's life should the child be born infected.

The joys of parenthood were replaced with fear.

That was why I wanted to get to Sanctuary City.

I feared for my son and my ability to care for him. Leah and I barricaded ourselves in our home; we failed to see what was going on in the world around us.

Yes, we knew about the Vee but we didn't know about society, because our area was overrun with Vee.

Sanctuary cities according to rumors were a success, and people left trails of hope along the way.

Something we didn't expect.

I held out hope that we weren't the only people who waited until the last minute to get to a sanctuary city and as the miles passed us, I saw evidence that there were others.

Not long after leaving the shed with my newborn son on the front seat, I saw a barn with a message spray painted on it.

Carver Town. Zee Free Zone. Stop before Sanctuary.

Like a rest stop sign on the side of the road, that barn gave me a destination.

Carver Town was about a little over a hundred miles ahead just across the state line.

I would stop, but would do so at a safe walking distance.

I didn't need to stop for me, I needed to stop for Edward.

If Carver Town was still a stopping point, perhaps there was a doctor or medical person there. I just needed someone to check the baby. To tell me he was going to be okay.

Joining up with someone wasn't a priority. In fact, I probably would venture alone, avoid others. Maybe only cross paths when looking for a place to rest or for supplies.

I couldn't just drive into a place like Carver Town, especially if there were people there. I couldn't. Not with Leah in the vehicle.

I couldn't leave her.

The smell of death was a frequent odor that could not be mistaken. All too often it permeated the air and served as a warning that an attack of the Vee was underway.

A mob smell was what I called it.

However, I never knew what the fresh smell of death was like until Leah had died. Twelve hours after her passing, she exuded a smell. It wasn't strong, a hint of sour, but a smell nonetheless I knew would only get worse in the closed in space of a car.

I likened it to opening a fridge and catching a whiff of something that just wasn't right.

Only this time, there was no closing the refrigerator door to stop it.

It was there, behind me as I drove. Of course, I chose to keep Leah. She kept following us, staggering, reaching out as if to say, "Why are you leaving me?"

She was my wife, the love of my life and I wasn't ready to give that up, or her.

Not yet.

The tape covered her mouth, her arms were bound and the seat belt kept her in place. The logical part of the brain was dead and undoing the belt in her state was like rocket science. She merely rocked back and forth never once reaching down and unhooking the belt.

I felt safe and didn't fear her getting free.

I had a little over a hundred miles and I would be out of our zone. I wasn't sure what was ahead, aside from Carver Town. There was no news or radio, nothing. Then again, everyone in our zone was either dead or evacuated. The roadways were barren and the only people I saw were Vees. It would be interesting to see what was in the next area. Maybe life… something.

A huge 'Welcome to West Virginia' sign created an arch on the highway as I entered the northern most part of the state. A mile later spray painted over the 'Visitor Station One mile' sign were the words, 'Sanctuary Info.'

Another hand-painted sign, this one was blue. It told me people were looking out for each other by leaving signs.

To me, things were looking brighter.

Carver Town.

Sanctuary information.

I worried that everything and everyone around us had died while we were held up in our house.

I wished they weren't exterminating the areas. Whatever that entailed. The Vee would eventually die off and expire. Our home was the best option and we'd had to leave it.

I debated on pulling over at the visitors' center until I saw there were no cars, no Vee. I parked out front of the visitor building, reached down and popped open the trunk.

Gently, I laid Edward on the passenger side floor, looked back at Leah, then opened my door. I peered around, then listened as best as I could for sound.

It was quiet and the only Vee I could smell was Leah.

Still, I couldn't be sure. In a 'ready to leave' position, hand holding onto my car door, I called out. "Hello!"

I waited.

Nothing.

"Hello."

With a third attempt, I beeped the horn. No Vee emerged, that was a good thing.

Staying diligent and focused, I hurried to the back of the car, opened the hatch and grabbed a blanket along with the baby carrier. It was one of those cloth things that strapped around your chest. One geared for newborns, it would keep Edward close to my chest, curled up and safe, allowing me to have my hands free.

Even though I saw no one around, I tossed the blanket over Leah to keep her hidden, figuring the tinted windows aided in that ask as well. I lifted Edward and placed him in the carrier. He squirmed some. Not much, then again, he was only a day old.

"It's okay," I told him. "We're safe."

There was no reason to go into the visitor center other than to seek out information. I needed to know what was ahead.

There were three cars in the parking lot all appearing to have been abandoned a while ago. The doors were open, windows smashed and the interior and paint was smeared with blood.

Body parts created a trail; they were so decomposed the flies didn't even show interest in them. I walked slowly to the building. One side of the double doors was open, the glass on the other had been smashed.

I was confident there were no Vee inside, because they would have come out when I made noise. That wasn't to say there weren't any in the area. I wanted to be fast in case they transcended on me.

A slaughter had taken place in that visitor center. Dried blood painted the walls, pools of it had hardened on the floor. The Vee left very little of their victims, hair, eyes, bones with tendons on them, maybe even a bit of muscle.

I had a brother who could put a chicken wing in his mouth and pull it out clean. That's what it reminded me of. Nothing was wasted.

Other than a human smorgasbord, it was once a place where people holed up. Probably traveling, saw the sanctuary information and stayed for the night. Canned goods and other food items were scattered about on the floor. I spotted a large backpack and lifted it. I would take those items. Even though Leah and I had packed the car, I didn't know if I would need more.

I didn't have time to dally and I looked around.

The entire place was nothing but a shrine to surviving.

On the far wall was a huge map of West Virginia, one of those 'you are here' jobs. Next to it was one of the United States. Circled on the map in thick marker were the areas of sanctuary cities. Along with notes on the map.

Avoid this route. Take this route.

A string was taped to a marker than dangled on the frame of the map. Written big on the wall was the instruction, 'Leave info for others that may pass through.'

People did and they left more.

John and Cindy Gray were there.

Melvin Hayes was looking for his daughter.

Along with factual speculation information about what was ahead.

Carver Town Vee Free

Bruceton infected

Heard I-79 was clear.

EAS reports highway blocked at mile marker nineteen.

When I saw that, I looked at the map. A blocked highway wasn't good. It meant I had to get off the highway either at Bruceton, the infected town, or before and take backroads to get to I-79. My gas situation was still good, but the loop around meant using more fuel. I could still make Carver Town, but there was now a chance I'd have to stop for the night.

The slight noise from my newborn son reiterated that.

I embedded the information I needed in my mind, then stuffed that backpack with things I'd need. I especially looked for bottled water. That was important for Edward and feeding him, keeping him clean. I would also check the cars outside for fuel.

Every little bit helped.

After I grabbed what I could from the floor, I lifted a map from the holder on the map wall and I walked out of the center.

As soon as we stepped outside, Edward started to fuss even more.

I had to change and feed him before I drove any further.

It was early, not even noon. I had a good six hours to get to Carver town or find a place for the evening.

It was doable.

RECALL

17 DAYS EARLIER

August 17

Early on, when we first hunkered down inside our house, only occasionally would scores of Vee mob outside, moving around in no particular order. It was as if they knew we were in there, but the journey up to the house was a bother.

At first they did. A few pounded relentlessly at our house. Then with simply blocking the windows and staying quiet, they moved on. Not far, but they were pounding on the house like a mini rerun of Night of the Living Dead.

After a week, they just moved on. They were still in the area, occasionally when we were really quiet we could hear an agonizing scream. Someone in the distance dying. The Vee were still finding people to attack.

We had become complacent.

Our home had a feeling of sanctuary. We lucked out, the Vee never returned to our neighborhood and we had no desire to leave. I made frequent trips out of the house to scavenge from the neighbors. Occasionally we'd venture out to be daring, to break the monotony and boredom. We had more than enough food and water.

Eventually the Vee would die off... eventually.

For the time being, the world was ours.

I kept trying the television after the programming ceased. Every day, twice a day just in case it returned.

Leah didn't bother or care to. She had her own routine. Surprisingly, we still had power and while we used minimal lights, she spent a lot of time in the back room, windows boarded and the small air conditioner running. The only room in the house with an air conditioner.

The constant hum of the cooling machine never garnished attention.

She kept the door closed and I loved going in there after the house got too stifling. Walking in was like a blast of refreshment to my entire body.

In her pregnant state, the heat made her hands and feet swell, so she needed to be cool.

Leah always looked peaceful. Either on the bed or in the rocking chair.

"Hey." I opened the door and walked in with a 'aw' of relief.

She was on the bed and looked up to me from her hardback journal, and smiled. "You're welcome to stay in here."

"No, you say that now," I said. 'But then you'll kick me out saying I am making the temperature go up."

She giggled.

I lay on the bed next to her. "I'm making food. Did you want to eat in here?"

"No, I'll come out. Let me finish this entry."

I tried to peek and she pulled it away.

"What?"

"You can't look. One day when I'm gone, you can read my thoughts. Until then..."

"Considering I'll be gone before you, you should let me see now."

"Cal, you'd be bored," she said. "Most of these are how I feel about the pregnancy. They've become more interesting lately though."

"I bet. I mean they can't be all that boring considering your pregnancy journal takes place in the middle of the apocalypse."

"It could be worse, Cal." She shut the journal, marking her spot with a pen. "We could be out there, lost, wandering, hiding… starving. Running for our lives."

"Without electricity," I added. "Yeah, we have quite the comfy apocalypse happening here."

"Yes, we do."

I rested my hand on her stomach, waiting to feel the baby move before I left. When I felt the thump against my fingers, I slowly sat up. "Well, I'll let you finish and make us something to eat."

"Thank you, I'll be right out."

I slipped from the bed and walked to the door and lingered there taking in the cool air for another moment. "Don't be too long."

"I won't."

I watched Leah open her journal and start writing again, I took that as my cue to leave.

Even though the world was dying around us, it was simple, calm and fear free in our home. I didn't take a single moment for granted, not one, because I also knew in the back of my mind, it wasn't going to last.

7

MARSHAL

September 3

We made it was far as Marshal, and I had to stop. It was during the drive that I realized newborns didn't really cry, they screamed and Edward did that constantly. He was hungry, I was aware of the problem, but I was so afraid to stop to tend to him.

I took the exit to avoid the blockade. All signs about sanctuary cities or for any help were gone. I saw nothing to indicate I was even on a safe route. I contemplated going back to look to see if the highway was really blocked.

There were no hand-painted signs, and like other places, there were no flyers lying on the ground from being dumped out of a plane.

Then again, only larger metropolises were told when to go, the rest of the country wasn't at risk of extermination.

Not by the government anyway.

What I did see were Vee. Groups of them, they didn't just stagger the streets, there were times I saw them at a building trying to get in. This told me survivors were there inside. The Vee were only relentless like that when they knew there was something they wanted.

It was an interesting ride.

Though Leah really didn't make any noise except for a low humming groan, I kept looking back in the rearview mirror at her. As if seeking some sort of approval from her. After a while, the glances became conversational looks, and I found myself talking to her.

"I know, I hear him," I said. "What can I do? I can't stop. I mean, I can, but stopping is more than pulling over. I have to check for safety. You've seen it out there. Okay, maybe you didn't. But there are Vee everywhere."

If she could talk, she'd probably berate me with guilt phrases. Why wasn't I taking care of our child? The baby was just born. I needed to man up, that sort of thing.

Finally, I did pull over to feed him. I did it fast and was pretty sure he didn't eat enough. I had to keep moving.

As if she were still my same Leah, I talked things out with her.

My talking to her wasn't so bad, at least I didn't imagine she answered me.

My life had been with Leah for a long time, and the previous couple of months it was just her and I. How could I not need and miss her? How could I not ignore what she had become? What would it hurt? I'd only do it for a little while. She was my best friend and I couldn't process that she was gone. It was hard to not believe in the shell of a dead body wasn't some semblance of her soul. It was still there in her eyes, I felt it.

Leah had only died a day earlier and in my heart and soul she wasn't gone yet. She was only quieter and looked different.

Then she got hungry.

Just outside of the town of Marshal she behaved differently, hunger was the only explanation I could come up with.

Leah started to thrash, her groaning turned into growls that were frightening. It grew louder each mile we drove. The sun wasn't even down yet, but I knew it was time to stop.

Marshal had life, and well, death.

The Vee roamed the streets and I saw homes that were fortified. I contemplated stopping at one of those, asking for help for me and my son, but decided against it. Truth be known, I had to deal with Leah.

From what I could tell Marshal was a farming town, or an old coal town. I didn't know which one, but it wasn't big. There wasn't a town square or main portion, it was just houses that were set far apart.

Most of them were a distance from the road and the Vee wandered the areas around the homes.

There were no stoplights, but there was a chain name gas station with a convenience store and I decided to make camp there.

I pulled the vehicle to the side of the building. I didn't see any Vee, none at all, but with Edward making all that noise it wouldn't be long. His screaming would be a dinner bell echoing in the quiet town. Every window in the convenience store was busted out. However, I had an idea.

Still wearing the carrier, I slipped Edward in against my chest and stepped form the car.

I opened the back door and grabbed the small duffel. It was the one that Leah and I deemed our night bag. It had a blanket, food and water. After shouldering that, then looking around for Vee, I headed into the dark convenience store.

It was rank, it had some sort of moldy smell to it and nothing was on the shelves. In fact most of them were overturned.

It wasn't safe in the main portion of the store, but that wasn't where I was headed.

When I was in college, I worked at a 7-Eleven, one of the jobs I hated was stocking the coolers. It was the sanctity of the cooler that I sought after. They always had a steel back door that had a safety latch so as not to get locked in. And though the doors to the coolers were glass the shelves were like a fence.

The area behind the shelves was roomy. I knew and figured it was our best option for the evening.

It wasn't hard, even in the darkened store, to find the door to the cooler. People had cleaned the shelves of every beverage so the smell was minimal.

The floor was concrete, there was plenty of room. I placed the duffle bag down and then Edward. He still screamed.

"I'll be right back. I promise," I told him.

I didn't want to leave him, but I had to.

I pulled the steal door closed, which muffled his noises and then headed back out of the store.

It was time to end the Leah saga, but I couldn't kill her. I just didn't have it in me to put down my wife.

When I walked back out to the car, she was thrashing even more. I knew I had to be fast. I opened her side of the door and then walked to the other side. Leaning in from there, I reached over and quickly pulled the tape from her mouth.

She snapped at me and did this demonic style scream.

My plan was to set her free. I knew I was chancing my supplies by leaving the car unlocked, but I had to let Leah go. I had to.

I hoped and prayed she would leave to find food and be gone. Then and only then could I face my loss and start to grieve.

Quickly, I reached out, pressed the red button and released the seat belt.

Once free she dove my way and I closed the door.

"I'm sorry, Leah," I said. "I love you."

She hadn't noticed her door was open and I seized my opportunity to turn back to the store.

I spun around only to see a large group of Vee coming my way.

I made my mad dash to the store only to see Leah stumble from the car. She turned to the oncoming Vee and did this cry out. It was frightening, almost as if she were communicating with them.

They moved at a good pace and just as I entered the store, so did they. The pursued me with hungry fervor. Even over the noise of the Vee I could hear Edward and I ran as fast I as I could toward the cooler.

When I reached that door, three Vee came at me from the back. I jumped in shock, opened the door and tried to shut it. Their arms reached through, stopping me from sealing it completely. I used all of my strength, putting my back into it to close it. I prayed in my mind for it to close. Three of them were hard, if any more reached in, we were doomed. I wouldn't be strong enough.

Finally, with a hard grunt, the door closed.

I looked down to see two severed arms on the ground. I shivered in disgust and kicked them away. Breathing heavily I caught my bearings and walked over to Edward. I picked him up from the ground, cradled him in my arms, and sat on the floor with my back against the wall.

The Vee attacked the steel door and then they gathered, hands pounding on the doors of the cooler.

I was surrounded, but I knew they wouldn't get in. I had to just wait it out. No matter how long it took because for the moment, my son and I were safe.

8

GOT YOUR BACK

September 4

When the way was clear and the last of the Vee vacated the store for something better, when the sky was light enough, I knew it was time to go. Last I looked at my gas gauge, I was teetering just under the half tank mark. It was time to put that last gas can in the tank. I needed to get us moving, try to get to Carver Town and head south after that.

What I really needed was rest. My head pounded, my mouth was dry, and my eyes were heavy. I tried to sleep the night before. I had ample time and opportunity, but I kept waking up. The nightmares were disturbing. I continuously dreamt that Edward had died, that he stopped breathing and I would lift his lifeless body to have him flop over my hands.

Each time I jolted awake, I checked him.

It was time to face the day and road ahead, and even more so, it was time to face the loss of Leah.

Edward was resting. Leaving him in that back cooler I quietly slipped out to pack the car and put in the last container of fuel.

I tried not to make any noise, I didn't need the Vee ascending on me. I gave great thought to each time I left the baby unattended. What would happen if I were attacked? I weighed the options and rather have the child die alone from starvation than torn to shreds with me.

The store was clear and I didn't see any Vee outside. My car seemed undisturbed and the back door was open.

I would be lying if I said I didn't look for Leah. She wasn't there and as I approached the vehicle I saw she wasn't inside.

I placed my backpack in the back seat, then carefully popped the hatch. I'd save shutting the doors for when I was ready to leave. Quickly, I grabbed the five gallon gas can and emptied the entire contents in the tank, all the while looking behind me for Vee. When finished, I placed the can back in the car and rushed into the store.

Edward wasn't crying and that was a good thing. I tossed the carrier over my shoulder and placed Edward in.

"It's okay little one, we're out of here."

I knew he didn't understand me, but I felt better talking to him.

Once again, I peeked for Vee before entering the store area. Seeing it was clear, I made a mad dash to the car. I grabbed my driver's door handle and stopped when from behind me, I heard the chamber engage on a weapon.

"Turn around," the male voice said.

"I'm not one of them," I replied.

"Hands up and turn around."

Slowly, I turned. I felt somewhat safe. After all, if he wanted me dead, why wouldn't he just shoot me?

A man stood before me holding a shotgun in my direction. His gray tee shirt was covered in blood, some of it looked dried. He was disheveled, but he didn't look injured. Obviously it was someone else's blood.

"I have a baby," I said. "A newborn. Please don't shoot."

"Be better for the baby if I did, now wouldn't it?" He lowered the aim.

"No!" I shouted nervously. "No. Please."

"I know you have gas in this thing. I watched you put it in," he said. "I would have been gone with it, but you have the keys. Hand them over."

"Look, we're just trying to get to Sanctuary City."

"What a coincidence. So am I. Give me the keys."

"Why don't we go together?" I asked nervously. "Really, I think…"

"Man, I heard that thing screaming all night. I'm not going anywhere with a noise maker. Now give me the keys."

"Okay, just let me get some supplies."

"You got three seconds."

"Just the baby supplies, let me get supplies to feed the baby."

He laughed. "One."

"They're in my back pocket."

"Two."

Trembling, I reached back for the keys and pulled them out, jingling them for him to see. For him to not get to number three. Chances were he was going to kill us anyhow. I believed it, but that was only briefly. I knew we'd be fine. In fact, I probably smiled.

"What the hell are you…?"

Leah.

In all her dead, half-naked glory, she stood behind the man and with a wide open mouth and plunged her teeth into the curve of his neck.

He screamed and I darted out of the way in case the gun went off. It didn't. He struggled to free himself, but blood poured down his chest as her jaws refused to let go.

I looked around for more Vee. Surely they'd come after that scream.

The man tumbled to the ground and as Leah dove on him, he released the shotgun.

I didn't have a gun, so I seized the moment and grabbed his. I'd worry about more ammunition later.

"Help me," he gurgled. "Help."

I knew the shotgun was engaged and I aimed it at him. That was my first thought, to spare his agony. My second thought was to spare Leah. Then I decided, shooting wasn't a smart thing. Not only would the noise attract Vee, I had never fired a shotgun. I didn't know what kind of kick it would have and Edward's safety was foremost. Did I want it to throw me back, holding my child and leave myself vulnerable.

The man on the ground, bleeding and dying didn't care about our well-being, why should I care about his?

I gave it a few seconds, mesmerized as Leah tore him apart.

He stopped fighting, his eyes remained open. He was gone. Leah kept chomping on him.

I headed to the driver's side, keys in hand, opened the door, tossed in the shotgun and started to get in. I'd drive off and then stop to close the back door and hatch.

After starting the engine, I put it in reverse gear, backed up, turned around and started to drive. I drove slowly, Edward still to my chest. I watched in the rearview mirror as Vee arrived behind me and started to encompass the man's body.

Leah stood, she walked away from him, leaving the others to devour his remains.

Two blocks away, seeing it was safe, I pulled over to close the back door and hatch. I was ready to leave when I saw her.

Leah was trying to reach us again.

"No," I groaned. "Please no, Leah."

What I needed to do was get in the car, give one more glance in the rearview mirror then mentally say goodbye to my wife.

Then again, I just couldn't leave her there. She would hurt someone else, and possibly be terminated by a stranger who didn't know her. Didn't love her. Didn't see the woman she was before.

I walked back to the car, removed Edward and placed him inside, then grabbed the shotgun. It was already engaged and, dangerous as it was, I figured I might as well fire off the round and make use of it.

End her suffering.

End my misery.

I aimed as she headed my way.

It broke my heart, it did. Even in her current form it was devastating to think about what I was going to do.

"I'm so sorry, Leah. So sorry. God forgive me." I pulled the trigger.

I was right about the kick. I wasn't ready for it and the force of the weapon knocked me back and off my balance. I landed on the ground.

When I looked up, Leah was still walking my way.

I didn't know if I missed or hit her, but I failed in putting her down.

Instead of trying again or driving away, I took that as a sign. I waited for her and would deal with it another time.

9

OREGON TRAIL

"She smells," Leah had told me. It was totally unlike Leah to say anything negative about anyone, except Marge Lemon. She was a co-worker of mine and Leah always had something to say about her when her name was brought up. That particular time was when I was getting names for a barbecue we were throwing. "She smells."

"Oh, she does not," I argued.

"She does. Like cat. How can you not smell that?"

"Really? Cat?"

"And Cal, have you ever noticed the way she eats? Things are always stuck in her teeth."

There were valid reasons why that conversation popped into my mind. The first was we had passed the exit for Lemon, West Virginia. The other was Leah herself.

"Look, Leah," I said to her in the back seat. "Lemon."

Leah was far from smelling like a rose. In fact, she was pretty bad. So bad that I pulled over at the self-serve car wash just outside of Marshal, busted into a vending machine and stole every single pine tree shaped air freshener in there.

There was her sour, rotting odor and then there was her mouth. It was still covered with the blood of the man who tried to carjack us, and his flesh filled her mouth. Leah chewed on it while staring ahead.

It was an odd and freaky sight.

"Marge has nothing on you," I looked in the rearview mirror. "Just sayin'."

What was wrong with me? I mean, really, what was going through my mind?

I was traveling with my two-day-old son, trying to get to a sanctuary city, with my decomposing, reanimated wife strapped in the back seat.

I think in my grief-stricken state it was like she was still with me, I hadn't lost her. Not yet. There was no shock and horror over her appearance, not that she looked normal, but she didn't seem to look as bad as any other Vee I had seen.

Again, that was probably my distorted perception.

When I pulled over to tend to Edward, I looked again at the map. I set a goal. A release goal. If Leah was still with me by the time I reached the welcome center on Interstate 79, then I would make her go.

I had to. How much further could I take her along?

The journey reminded me so much of a game I used to play as a child. It was called, *Oregon Trail*. A poor-graphic game that made the player plan out a survival trip during the westward expansion. You put in your name, the members of your family, and with an allotted amount of money, the player would purchase enough supplies to get his family from Kansas to Oregon alive and well.

Usually, it didn't work out. The route was rough and dangerous. Along the trail the virtual family got ill, the wagon petered out, the food stolen. Everything and anything happened. The game would flash a screen and you'd just continue on.

You broke a wagon wheel.

Mary broke a bone.

Mary has typhoid.

Mary has died.

For me, the signs along the way and the events that occurred created a live version of that game from the moment I left the house. All I needed was the bad music.

Leah has been bitten.

Leah gave birth.

Leah has died.

Sanctuary Trail.

Next stop, Carver Town. Did you want to look around?

No. Hell no.

Carver Town may have been Vee free at one time, but I didn't need to walk in to know it no longer was a safe zone.

My plan was to pull over and hide the car a mile or so before Carver. I would have done so had I not seen that lone Vee walking the road. Something told me he wasn't turned away at the gate by some guy saying. "Hey now, we're a Vee free zone, just turn it around buddy."

Hordes of dead roamed in front of the 'We are Vee Free' sign, as if gloating that they were victorious.

Even though I didn't need to stop, I did however, have no choice but to drive through it. I was glad I did.

The main road in town was like navigating a video game. Vee bombarded the car, pounding relentlessly. Twice I swore I heard someone yelling out for help. It wasn't safe and I couldn't stop. However, I did see another piece of my proverbial *Oregon Trail*.

Safe Route to Sanctuary 14, 15, 16 use Highway 119.

I didn't know how old that sign was or how much credence I should put into it, but it was worth a shot to try. It was either Highway 119 or the main interstate. Since doing my calculations and finding I would need at least one more full tank to get there, I figured I stood a better chance of refueling on the safe route.

10

CLEANLINESS

Highway 119 was a wide stretch of secondary artery that ran south in West Virginia. It was darted with small towns, occasional houses and businesses along the route.

A truck actually passed me on that road not long after I hit it.

I was not alone.

I wasn't the only one headed to a sanctuary city.

I picked up the pace to try to catch the black Ford, but they were flying. Fearing that I'd lose control of the vehicle with my son in the car, I slowed down. Eventually, I figured I'd catch him.

Plus, speeding wasted gas and I didn't have it to spare.

Truth was if I didn't find gas within the next hour or two, I was not making it much further.

Then about forty miles in, I saw the black truck again. It was pulling out of a gas station on the other side of the highway.

It cut across the lanes and continued south.

Did he or she not even see me? They seemed to be in that every man for himself mode. Then again, weren't we all?

I wondered if the station had power, how he got gas, if he even did. There was one way to find out and I veered across the highway to that service station.

No sooner did I enter the lot than an older woman carrying a rifle walked out. For some reason I worried that she would shoot Leah. That was stupid and silly, but my gut jumped in nervousness and I was glad my rear windows were tinted.

Edward was quiet. I removed the carrier from my body, laid him on the passenger's seat, then opened my door and raised my hands.

"I don't mean any harm," I said. "I just need gas."

She was a stout woman in her sixties; she held the rifle steady and with confidence. "Where are you headed?"

"Sanctuary City…" I paused. "Sixteen."

"Sixteen? I haven't seen anyone headed there in a while. You from Boston?"

"Philly."

She nodded. "You can put your hands down."

I did.

"You're half way there, you know."

"I know. And I really think one full tank will get me there."

"I can't fill you up. I can't. Only reason I am here is to help people who want to go to a sanctuary city. I got to make what I have last. I can trade you some fuel. What do you got?"

"I have food and water…"

She shook her head. "I have that. Right now going price is medicine or weapons. The medicine has got to be worth it."

"I have ibuprofen." I shifted my eyes to my car. "I have… I have a shotgun. But I don't have any ammunition."

"You're riding around with a weapon you can't fire?"

"I think there's one more round in there. Not sure."

"Let me see."

I walked around to the passenger side and opened the door. When I grabbed the shotgun, Edward squalled.

"What is that?"

"My son. He's a newborn. My wife died giving birth." I handed her the shotgun.

"You're toting a newborn?" she asked.

"I have to. I have to get him to sanctuary."

She examined the shot gun. "Alright. This will do." She turned and walked back inside. When she returned she had a five gallon container and she set it down by my legs. "About seventy miles south there's a church. Ravenswood. They let people rest there. Another twenty is Berchum Mills, he has property that he'll trade a safe night's rest for food and water. Lots of places in between."

"Thank you," I said. "Are you headed to a sanctuary city?"

"No." She shook her head. "I'm gonna take my chances out here."

I lifted the gas can. "Thank you again."

"Listen, try to make it as far as you can. It's not safe out there. It really isn't. There's more and more of those things daily."

"I know."

"Just be careful. Godspeed to you."

I began to carry the gas can and stopped. "Do you... do you know anything else?"

"What do you mean?"

"I mean, I haven't heard the news in weeks."

"You probably know about as much as me," she said. "There hasn't been any news. I only hear what people tell me. Big cities are overrun. Not so much out this way. Used to be the infection wasn't anywhere near here. Now... the Vee free zones get smaller by the day."

"Why do you think that is? A wave hits?"

"It's been a while since one of those came. This thing is every-where now, no more need for nature to spread it. To answer your question, we were Vee free until people came through infected and turned. That's the way it is everywhere I suppose."

"I suppose. Thank you again." I could have placed the can in the back of the car, but I decided to add it all to the tank. I returned her can, got in my car, placed on the carrier Edward was in and started the car. I sighed out in relief. I had nearly a full tank. I could make it and if Edward was cooperative, I could do so without having to stop.

<><><><><>

So, this is what you look like when you expire.

That was my thought when I pulled over into the parking lot of a beer distributor about eight miles after I left Gas Can Lady.

There was something off about our final moments. She watched me leave, but she did so as if she was looking for something. It left me with a bad feeling and I wouldn't have stopped had Edward not been out of hand.

I had to pull over and take a break. Stop moving. I did what I normally did when I left the car. I opened the back door and unbuckled Leah. Each time I did that I hoped that she would leave and I wouldn't have to be the one to deal with it.

I just wanted badly to acknowledge her death, mourn her and be sad. I couldn't. She was there, always there. Even in her Vee state she was still my wife. Little by little she took on a Vee look. Her skin seemed to shrink like a raisin, although it looked as if underneath the layers of skin fluid was waiting to ooze out. The area under her eyes were dark and sunken in. Her pupils were glazed over and gray.

The eyes were unmistakable.

He had the eyes. The man in the beer distributor. Without a doubt he was a Vee. Aside from the eyes, his fingers had that boney look with the black fingernail beds. There were no shoes on his feet and his soles were split from walking. He was on the floor, his upper body slanted and propped against the Bud Light Beer display, his legs extended out and he didn't move.

He was probably infected in a wave because there were no visible bite marks, no organs torn from his body. There was no gunshot wound or bashed in skull.

Nothing.

Yet, he was dead... again.

It was a Vee appearance I had never seen. His toes were curled and feet pointed inward, his hands were atrophic and tight to his body.

His skin looked dry, mummified, and his wide open mouth formed an 'O' trying the impossible to gasp for air.

I had heard that they could just drop and cease to exist. Beer Vee Man was proof. I nudged his leg with my foot and when I did a huge, brown water bug crawled out of his mouth and dropped to his lap.

Clutching Edward, I jumped back and cringed.

Of everything I had seen, who would have thought a bug bothered me. I stayed until Edward was soothed, and I grabbed some beer. Not just for myself, but possibly for a trade, within a couple hours I was back on the road. I probably wouldn't make it to Sanctuary Sixteen, not on this day, but I was close.

There were things I thought of and things I didn't. I read enough beforehand to have survival supplies. Enough to get me to Sanctuary and beyond. My journey was met mainly with Vee trouble and blocked roads. I couldn't take for granted that there wouldn't be trouble with humans ahead. After nearly having my car stolen earlier, I couldn't take a chance that it would happen again.

When I spotted the church with the fence around it, I backed up out of sight and pulled the car off to the wooded side of the road, parking it as if it were abandoned. Leah got out and faced the woods. I locked the doors, placed a backpack on my shoulder and the carrier on my chest.

Hurriedly, I moved from Leah. While she had not tried to attack me yet, I couldn't take the chance and luckily she didn't move all that fast.

Once I was at a distance, I stopped and watched her move into the woods.

She didn't follow me. My heart sunk. It was goodbye, and the church was the sure sign that I was to begin my process of letting go.

I walked the near half-mile distance and as I closed in, I saw several Vee moving around the fence.

I could move by them but only if the fence was unlocked.

I kept the hammer in the backpack and pulled it out. I didn't have a clue how I would fight them off with Edward strapped to my chest, but I would try and be careful about it. Edward was a newborn and delicate.

"Let me get to the church, please let me get us there," I spoke softly, focusing on the fence.

The Vee spotted me and made their way towards me. I darted out of the way of the first one, shoved the next and picked up the pace to the fence. There was one there, a female, standing by the gate as if she were on guard.

I lifted the hammer, I would have to try, I had to get in. The moment I raised it, an arrow sailed into the Vee's head and she dropped. Surprised by that, I spun to see a priest headed my way. At least he looked like a priest. A stout older man who wore all black and rushed to the fence to unlock it.

"Come on in," he said.

"That was impressive shooting," I told him.

"Yes, well, in these times you have to be." He waited for me to step through and he closed and locked the gate. "Pastor Jim."

"Calvin. My name is Calvin. Thank you."

He nodded then his eyes shifted to the carrier. With Edward nestled in there, I guess it was hard to see if it was a baby or supplies.

"My son. He was born two days ago."

"Oh my. Then you hold a miracle. Let's get you in there."

"Thank you."

Pastor Jim extended his hand, directing me to the church. It was a short walk across the parking lot. A large structure with white siding, surrounded by beautiful bushes and eight concrete steps that led to the red double doors.

"I appreciate this," I said as he opened the doors. "It's very kind of you."

"All are welcome in God's house. I wanted it to be that way, so we erected those fences early on. I was ready to leave, then when people were passing on their way to different sanctuaries needing help I knew I couldn't leave."

The double doors led right into the church and the second I entered, people turned and looked at me. There had to be at least a dozen. Some looked like they were right at home.

"Are all these people travelers?"

"Some. Some lost their homes in Carver or were overrun. They're waiting it out until this thing is over."

"They drop you know?"

"What do you mean?" he asked.

"The rumors about how they can just drop and die for good. They're true. I think. I saw one that wasn't shot."

"Well that's encouraging." He cleared his throat. "You look like you need to clean up."

"Actually, I do. I suppose I don't smell all that good either."

"Well, smelling bad keeps the Formers away. But in here... there are none. So..." he smiled. "There's a room behind the sanctuary. Barrels of water for cleaning. I'll show you where it is so you can wash up."

"Thank you."

"Are you hungry?" he asked.

"No, I'm good. Thanks."

"This way."

Pastor Jim led me up the aisle of the church. I nodded and gave a closed mouth smile to people that I passed as I followed him. He took me to a back room, closing the door and leaving me and Edward to our privacy.

The room was pretty large with a conference table and a couch. I wouldn't have exactly labeled the bins of water as 'barrels,' but they were deep and filled.

There was a small basin on the chest of drawers and a pitcher that I assumed was used to fill the basin. It was a welcome relief to be in such a clean environment. I wanted to throw out my clothes after I washed up, but I didn't bring anything extra. After I had washed up, I then unraveled Edward and gently washed his skin. At first I thought he enjoyed it and then he started to whimper. Those whimpers transformed into full blown newborn screams. There was nothing I could do to calm him down.

We weren't in there very long, maybe a half hour or so, when Pastor Jim knocked on the door and entered. I was swaying the baby in my arms in an attempt to silence him, but he wouldn't quiet down.

"Cal, I came to…" He paused, staring.

"What? I'm sorry. I'm trying to calm him. He won't…"

"You can't stay. You must leave. I'm sorry, take him and go." He turned.

"Wait. Why?"

"This is a quiet place. We can't take a chance of the Formers hearing and trying…"

"You have a fence."

"It won't hold if too many show up. I'm sorry. We don't want you here."

"Whatever happened to all are welcome in God's house?"

Pastor Jim wouldn't even turn around. "Don't make us take you out. It would be best if you left through the back door."

He couldn't even look at me. Of course not, he was sending an innocent baby out into the madness. I felt horrible for my son. To be so young and not be wanted.

It wasn't going to be long before the sun would start to set. I hurried and grabbed my things and left, as requested, through the back door. I didn't have time to beg or argue. I had to take Edward, get back on the road and find shelter before nightfall.

11

OUST

It would actually be quite comical if it wasn't so pathetic and sad, how Leah kept following us and coming back like some sort of stray cat. It was hilarious if she knew. There was no way, no how, she did. It had to be instinct.

I let her in the car. About the twenty mile mark, as it often did, Highway 119 transformed into a two lane road to pass through a small town. This one consisted of a car repair shop and a volunteer fire department. Just as we hit the edge of town, I saw the property of Berchum Mills. Or I guessed it was his.

A long sloped driveway from the road led up to a two-story frame house and a barn.

I could see people moving around on the property, at least I hoped they were people. Before we were spotted, I hid and locked the car and forced Leah out.

"Go, Leah, just go. I have to get Edward safe. Go," I told her then took off with Edward down the road.

Not only was Edward a newborn, I knew he wasn't doing well. He wasn't taking his bottle and if it didn't come back out of his mouth, it went right through him. More than ever I had to get him to Sanctuary City, at least for medical help.

Stopping wasn't an option, it was a must. It was getting dark.

My backpack was still full of supplies and bartering items. I made it to the driveway with ease, checking once to make sure Leah didn't follow. Half way up, a truck blocked the driveway and a man stood outside of it.

"Stop," he instructed. "What do you want?"

"I was told this was a safe place to stop for the night. I need to rest."

"That a baby?" he asked.

I nodded. "My son. He's two days old."

"I'll let you through. I don't think Mr. Mills is going to let you stay though."

"Why not?"

"They make noise. At night, sound travels. May not look it, but there are a lot of those things around."

"Can I ask him?" I asked. "I mean, let me talk to him."

The man lifted a walkie-talkie to his mouth. "Hey, got a guy here. Needs a place to stay. He wants to talk to you. He has a baby."

There was a hiss of static. Then, "Send him up. I'll meet him at the gate."

"You heard," the man said. "Head straight up. He'll be the big guy waiting up there."

"Thank you. Thank you so much," I said.

"Don't thank me. I'm just filtering people."

I understood and made my way up the driveway.

Sure enough, a big guy stood there. He wore a green baseball cap and a checkered shirt. He opened the fence and stepped out to greet me.

"Mr. Mills?" I asked.

"Yep." He lifted his chin. "How old is that baby?"

"Two days."

"I see."

"We're trying to get to Sanctuary Sixteen and—"

"He's not crying."

"He's sleeping."

"A newborn?" he asked, then stepped forward and peeked at Edward.

"See."

"I do. You can't stay here."

"We won't be any trouble. I know—"

"Son, there shouldn't be a baby in this godforsaken world, you know that."

"He's my child. My wife died giving birth to him. What was I supposed to do, just leave him?"

"I hear you, but people in your same situation made a humane choice."

"I know what you're saying. What you're implying. Humane. Why make him live in this world? What kind of life can he have?"

"Jesus, that is—"

"I have to try. I do," I interrupted him and pleaded. "For my wife. For… Edward. That's his name. I have to try."

"I can't let you in here. I have people that live here, waiting this thing out. We're safe here. We don't need the infected to make their way in. Our perimeters aren't that strong."

I looked over his shoulder to the people there. Tents were erected, there were men and women. I even spotted a young girl. They all watched me talking to him.

"Please. I'll leave at first light. I promise."

Mr. Mills looked at me and sighed out heavily. "The barn is not in the fenced area, but it will give you shelter."

"Thank you."

"Look. I can't make promises. If there is a lot of crying, scream-ing… I can't promise what people might do. Any noise is a risk."

"I understand. Thank you again for at least giving me a chance."

He pointed to the barn and I walked toward it. It never once dawned on me that people would see an innocent baby as such a risk. Maybe I would feel the same if I were in their position.

I vowed right then and there, it was the last time I'd beg someone for a place to stay and be safe. If I had to stop again before Sanctuary City, I would handle things myself. Find my own shelter. I didn't want to be in the position where someone would turn me and my son away and make us feel less than human.

<><><><><>

I never expected to be in that position. Leah was supposed to be there, be the one to help me with the baby when he became out of control. I even thought about that video I saw, the magic baby cure to silence any baby.

It didn't work.

It was unbearable and frustrating, as the night moved in, his whimpers and screams seemed louder.

There was no doubt, even though we were in that barn, all noises echoed across the land of Mr. Mills.

To add to it all, every few minutes, I'd hear a whispering voice. Not a soft soothing voice, but angry.

"Shut it up."

"Silence it, or I will!"

I sat on the ground, rocking him back and forth, my only light was one of those little circle battery operated jobs. What was wrong with him? Was he hungry? Cold? Sick?

"Please, Ed, please be quiet. Please."

"We're warning you."

Suddenly I was overcome with this horrendous fear for myself and my child. There were more voices yelling at me and Edward screamed louder.

"Shh. Shh." I stared at him, my body trembling. I tried putting a bottle in his mouth, he didn't want it. I didn't know what to do.

I found my hand covering his mouth, muffling his noise. Then as my blood pressure rose and heart pounded faster, my hand pressed tighter covering his mouth and nose.

He struggled, and I just kept it there.

Oh my God. What was I doing? Was I killing my own child because I was scared of the others outside? What was wrong with me?

I lifted my hand at the same time the barn door flew open with a bang.

It was hard to see who was there. I saw four figures.

"You were warned," the one voice said.

"No. I'll keep him quiet." I stumbled to a stand and backed up.

The four of them rushed at me.

I moved quickly, but someone stepped on the light, making the barn completely dark. I could see a hint of light from outside the barn doors and aimed that way. When I did, I felt the strike to my face. Was it a fist? The hit sent me flying back. I clutched Edward as tight as I could and caught my balance before I hit the ground.

Again, I tried to run, but the barn doors shut and it was all black. My eyes didn't have time to adjust when I felt Edward ripped from my arms. His cries continued and faded.

"No!" I cried out. "No!"

My scream was quickly silenced when I felt the object slam into my gut, knocking the wind from me.

All I could think about was my son, my poor son. I couldn't even hear him anymore. I landed hard to the ground and the blows started one by one. A strike to my gut, my legs, my head. They only stopped when one of them grabbed me, pulled me by my shirt and dragged me for the longest time. I was pulled from the smooth hay covered floor of the barn to outside. The rough terrain scraped painfully against my body. When they finally tossed me aside, the pummeling began again.

It didn't matter though. I closed my eyes and waited for death. What was the point of fighting? I failed. Edward was gone.

12

SAVING GRACE

September 5

When I opened my eyes, all I could see was the crushed fallen leaves. It was light out and I was on my stomach. A simple movement of my hand shot a danger of pain through my entire body. My eye sight was blurred and my lips were so swollen they were tight. I attempted to run my tongue over my teeth, but when I did, I felt them resting in my mouth. It took a lot, but I lifted my head and spat. A blood clot emerged, followed by a long strand of blood filled saliva, along with several teeth.

It was hard to pinpoint where I hurt, because everything hurt.

Then reality hit me.

Edward. Where was he?

A saddened and aching moan seeped from me as I clutched the ground in an attempt to stand. My legs buckled and I fell back to the ground.

Oh, God, no. Not my son.

I had to get it together, think of him and not myself.

I cringed and grunted to regain my stand and fought my hurt and wobbling legs. I wondered if maybe I was dead. Maybe I had turned into one of them. I glanced down to my hand; it trembled and then, just to make sure, I tried to speak.

"Edward," I said softly. Then I closed my eyes tight. The emotional pain was more than the physical. If I did anything, I had to find my son.

I didn't even know where I was. I was surrounded by trees. No matter where I looked, I couldn't see anything but those trees.

I held up my wrist to see my watch. It was hard to focus and I knew that the time of eleven-twelve wasn't nighttime. My God, I had been unconscious for twelve hours.

If I did find Edward, chances were there'd be nothing left.

The loss of leaves allowed me to look at the sky. We were headed south and I looked for the sun to get my direction. I headed to where I believed was south. Every step I took hurt, but I kept going.

About twenty feet into my walk, I saw blood and the leaves were pressed and scattered. The muddy ground had footprints, lots of them. Peering around, I saw a trail. I wasn't a tracker, and didn't need to be one to know that was where they dragged me.

My best recourse was to follow that dragging trail and go back to the barn, that's where they took Edward from me. As I staggered, my chest felt heavy and I could hear my own wheezing breath. My head throbbed and burned. I reached up to feel a huge gash. It was still damp and when I looked down, my shirt was saturated with blood. I was hurt in so many places, I was probably dying.

Fueled by emotions and determination, I kept going, stumbling, getting back up. I knew they dragged me for a long time, I just didn't realize how far.

The trees thinned out as I entered more of a clearing. I tripped over the uneven ground and toppled back down again. I rolled over and got to all fours. It was when I started to stand that I saw it.

I was headed south and it was back in the trees, far off the path I was taking.

It may have been far, my eyesight was blurry, but there was no denying that Edward's infant carrier hung from a branch by the shoulder strap.

My adrenaline shot up and I moved with more of a rush to get to that carrier. I was fueled, I didn't even notice the pain anymore. My mind cried, *No No No* as I made it to the tree.

I lifted my arm to grab the carrier and my entire side felt aflame. I took a deep breath, grabbed on to the end of it and pulled. With grunts of pain and all my strength, I managed to free it and the carrier fell.

I caught it before it hit the ground.

It was empty.

My beating heart sunk to my stomach as I dropped to my knees.

The strap had a bloody hand print on it and I brought the carrier to my face.

At first I whimpered the agony of my loss, then with my head arched back, holding that carrier, I cried out deep and long. One gut wrenching cry of sorrow. I didn't care who heard me. In fact, I wanted them to.

I wanted to die. Maybe if I was lucky the Vee would come. If they didn't, I'd find my way to the road and wait for them to come.

Allow the Vee to consume my body and my pain.

Why live?

I took a few deep breaths, inhaled again to scream but didn't.

A young girl stood on a slight crest about twenty feet from me, holding a baby blanket.

I stood up.

She brought her index finger to her mouth as if to signal me to be quiet, then she turned and disappeared over the grade.

I wanted to call out, "Wait" but she needed me not to make a noise, and believing she had found my dead son, I followed her.

When I arrived where she had stood, I looked down. She was at the bottom of a hill. I could tell by the way she held the blanket she was holding a baby.

More than likely, Edward.

I slid down that small hill more so than walked, and tripped my way to her.

She had a young face, that of someone that wasn't even a teenager, but she was tall. Her long dark blonde hair was pulled into a messy ponytail. Her face was dirty and her hands... bloody.

To me, she was far too young to blame for Edward's death. More than likely she was walking and found him. I remembered seeing her when I arrived at the gate to Mr. Mills' home.

At least, I'd hold Edward one more time.

I reached out for the blanket. When my fingers touched him, his bare arm shot out of the blanket and his fingers curled.

I gasped.

He was moving? Edward was moving? I grabbed the blanket with him and he squirmed in my arms. I opened the blanket to see my naked son and his legs kicked.

"How?" I covered Edward and held him close to my body. I tried not to cry, I couldn't even form a sentence. "How? I thought…"

"I heard them talking last night. Planning." Her voice quivered. "How they were going to kill you and take your stuff. I couldn't… it was a baby."

"You were there?"

She nodded. "I grabbed him from you and ran."

I closed my eyes. "Thank you."

"I had to take his sleeper off," she said. "I covered it with blood. Your blood and told them, I crushed his skull. I hid him here and then came back."

Edward fussed and moved a little, but that was it. I didn't see any injuries.

"He's quiet," I said.

"I… I fed him for you."

My shoulders bounced and I fought back the tears. "I can't thank you enough." I fumbled placing the carrier over my shoulder. In fact, I could barely lift my shoulder. I hated not holding Edward, but I had to move. "I have to go. Get him dressed."

"They took all your stuff. I went to the barn, all that was there was a bottle."

"That's fine." I turned left to right. "Do you know which way to get to the road?"

"There's a stream over the next hill." She pointed in that direction. "Cross it and keep going straight. You'll see it."

"Thank you." I started to walk.

"They took your stuff."

I reached for my front pocket, and felt my keys. I had moved them there because they hurt to sit on. "Not everything." If it didn't hurt to smile, I would have.

It was time to move forward, follow her direction.

"Mister," she called me. "You're headed to Sanctuary City, right?"

"One of them, yes."

"Can I come with you?"

I stopped walking. "No, that's not a good idea. You should go back there."

"But you're hurt," she said.

"I'll be fine." I started walking again.

"You should stop at the creek to wash your cuts."

"I'm fine."

"I can help you."

Again, I stopped. "I said I'd be fine."

"You don't look fine. You're all beat up and bleeding still."

I kept walking.

"I can be a big help. I know this area really good."

"You should stay back. Go now, before you're missed," I said.

"No one's gonna miss me. They ain't all that good there. The people I mean. They're getting worse waiting on the transport guy. I'm… I'm afraid."

"Somehow I doubt that."

"I saved Edward!" she shouted.

I spun around. "How did you know his name?"

"I heard you tell Mr. Mills. I saved him. I stopped them men from crushing him. Don't that mean anything? I don't want to go back there."

"How do you know I'm all that good?"

"Because you ain't killed her yet." She extended her arm and swung out a point to her left.

My shoulders dropped.

Leah was standing there.

13

PARTNER

Her name was Hannah and she had this innocent yet intelligent air about her. She carried a Barbie backpack, even though she seemed too old for one. I don't know what all she had in there, it was packed to the gills.

At the creek she pulled out a sock for me to use as a cloth.

"That's okay, I have a whole pack. My mom said socks can be used for a lot of different things." She handed me the sock, then took Edward while I cleaned up.

I dampened the sock in the creek, raised my eyes to her then shifted them to Leah who kept her distance. Her head was tilted, her hair dangled and even at a distance, I could see she was covered with blood.

"How did you know?" I asked.

"About her?" She looked at Leah. "Mr. Mills talks with his radio all the time. Pastor Jim radioed and said a man carrying a baby might be stopping by. Said he watched you leave the church and you were lugging a former. Those were his words, not mine."

I winced in pain as I brought the water to my head.

"I was gonna watch out for you. You know, look for you coming. Nothing else to do up there. But you got there so fast. No one ever walked that stretch that fast. So I ran to the far end of the fence to peek. Sure enough she was tagging behind. She ain't got no pants on, you know. Her lady parts are showing."

"I know."

She reached in her backpack and handed me another sock. "Don't keep washing with dirty ones. You're just moving the dirt and blood. You might get infected."

"If I don't die from these injuries first."

"Or mebas."

"What?" I laughed.

"Mebas. My mom didn't let us play in the creek. She always told us not to 'cause there are mebas in there."

"Amoebas," I corrected.

"Same thing."

"Okay."

"Anyhow, she says they're all in the creek and lakes and if we get one, our flesh will come off."

"Swell. Back to what we were talking about. Did anyone mention about how fast I got there?" I asked.

Hannah shook her head. "They probably figured Pastor Jim just waited to radio. Don't forget to wash your arms, they're all scraped up."

"Thanks."

"Who is she?"

I lowered my head. "My wife. She died after she gave birth."

"Well that makes sense why she's not wearing no pants."

"Yeah," I partially smiled, but stopped when it burned. "You're not scared of her?"

"Not really. Not yet. She's moves slow."

"I know."

"Plus. She's good now. She got one of them guys that beat you. The more they get in them, the longer the calm ones are calm. At least that's what I learned."

"You're a plethora of information."

"I don't know what that means," she said.

"It means you know a lot of stuff."

"I do. About this I do. I listen."

"How old are you?" I asked.

"Twelve. Well, I'll be twelve... what's the date?"

I looked down at my watch. "September fifth."

Hannah sat up straight. "I'll be twelve in two days." She then curled her lip and titled her head. "Not a fun way to spend your birthday, huh?"

"Well, if all goes well. If I don't die... from mebas... you'll spend your birthday in a sanctuary city. That won't be too bad, will it?"

"Does that mean I can come with you?"

"Yes," I replied, and soaked the sock again. "You can come."

Hannah smiled.

14

SPUTTER

It had only been a couple days, but it was good to have someone else to talk to, even if she made my head spin.

When we emerged onto the road, I ignored her telling me that we were going the wrong way because I knew soon enough she would see why.

"Don't know why we're walking this way. This road takes you pretty close," she said.

"Trust me, Hannah. I know what I'm doing. How long were you with Mr. Mills?"

"Three weeks. I was supposed to go when the transport man returned. I don't know when they would come."

"What is a transport man?" I asked.

"He trades things for a ride. He has a big old cart and four horses. Takes four days to get to sanctuary."

"Horses and a cart. Wow. Oregon Trail."

"What? Is that where we're headed?"

"No."

"'Cause either way we're walking the wrong way."

I kept telling her, "You'll see."

And she did.

The moment she knew we were getting in the car, she jumped with joy and giggled... a lot.

"Does this have enough gas?" she asked.

"I think so. If not, we'll get close and I have supplies."

"Oh, wow, Calvin, that was good thinking to hide it."

"I know."

I freed the car from my hiding place and pulled out onto the road. Hannah jumped in the front seat and I paused before climbing in, "Listen, Hannah, I can't... I can't leave her yet."

"Who?"

I pointed to Leah who staggered up the road.

"You aren't bringing me along to feed her when she gets crazy, are you?"

I shook my head. "No. I won't let her hurt you."

Hannah nodded and I got inside.

"You gonna drive with Edward on your chest?"

"I have been?"

She held out her hands. "I don't mind. I'll strap him to me."

"You sure?" I lifted the carrier from me and handed him to her.

By the time we were ready to pull out, Leah arrived at the car.

I debated at that moment to drive off. I really did, but I couldn't bring myself to do it. I got out, opened the door and Leah crawled in. I strapped her down just in case.

"You have her trained," Hannah said. "I always knew the calm ones had some left over smarts."

"What do you know about the calms ones?" I asked as I drove off.

"I first heard about them on the news. They called them something. Some technical term. The ones that got sick from being bit. The ones that turned in the wave are the ones that are the worst.

"Yeah, I know. Have you seen many calm ones?"

Hannah nodded. "Can I have one of these?" She pointed to the air freshener.

"Yes, why."

"I don't know if you noticed it really stinks in here." She brought the air freshener to her nose. "What did you ask me?"

"What you knew about the calm ones."

"Oh, yeah. Most of the time, you get bit you don't survive enough to turn. Or you do and you're so tore up you can't get back up, then you become a twitcher. Just kinda lay there in this puddle of mush, all twitchin', like Mr. Davis my third grade teacher."

Again, she made my head spin.

"My mom got tore up pretty good. My dad put down my brother."

"I'm sorry, Hannah, I am. How long ago was it?"

"A while. Maybe a month. We were in Carver Town."

"Is that where you're from?"

"No. I'm from Morgantown."

"Is that how you know the area?" I asked. "You said you know the area really well."

"I do. Been to Carver Town a lot. When my home got hit, we heard from my cousin that Carver Town was good and so we went there because we had family there. They shut the town down. It was normal. Everyone was normal. The one guy said 'cause it was secluded and hidden that no wave could hit there. After a few weeks, my dad and uncle went all up and down the highway posting signs saying there weren't no Vee."

"What happened? Did a wave actually hit?"

"No," Hannah said. "A bunch just came over the hills and into town. There were hundreds. We got in the car, my mom, dad, brother and baby sister, but we got surrounded. My dad got bit, they broke through the windows. My mom was yelling, 'get out the sunroof Hannah, help your brother.' So I did. I grabbed for my brother, but the Vee were in the car. My baby sister was in the car seat, there was nothing left."

"What about your brother?"

"They pulled him and ate him. By the time I got him to the roof he was only half left."

"Oh my God. Hannah, that's terrible. I am so sorry you went through that."

"Some guys came and shot them so I could get free, but it was too late. My mom, brother and sister were dead. My dad didn't die. He put down my brother before he could turn into one. My dad and I hid in a hardware store. Until he died."

"Did he turn into a Vee?" I asked.

"Yep and… that's how I really knew about the calm ones and why I know you're letting her follow you. My dad followed me."

"Really?"

"I wasn't like you," she said. "I didn't have a car and I had to walk. He followed me, I just couldn't kill him."

"Did he ever try to hurt you?"

"Oh, sure, lots of times. I could always outrun him and he always found something else to attack. Then he'd follow me again."

"What happened to him. Did you..."

"No." She shook her head. "Pastor Jim put him down. I was walking up to his gate and he put an arrow in him. I cried. He thought it was because I was happy to be safe. I cried because it was my dad."

I felt horrible for her. She had been through so much.

"You're really brave," I told her.

"What are you going to do with her?"

"I don't know. A part of me knows it isn't her anymore. Yet, when I look at her all I see is my wife. Even in the physical state she's in."

"Do you want to be the one to do it?" Hannah asked.

"You mean put her down?"

Hannah nodded.

"I'd like to be the one. I just don't know if I have it in me. If I did, I don't know how I would do it."

"You don't have a gun?"

"I did. For like a minute. I traded it for gas."

"You traded your only weapon for gas?"

"Yeah, I mean I haven't had problems with the Vee since back home." I watched as Hannah took another long whiff of the air freshener. "Maybe once I get close to sanctuary I'll find a way to lose her."

"What about Edward?" she asked. "What if it's like Mr. Mills' and they don't let you in with him?"

"Oh, they have to. He's a baby, right? It's a different set up than Mr. Mills' place. I'm sure of it. Out here, while we're traveling, I'm going to have to be more careful."

She nodded and looked down to Edward then sniffed the air freshener again. We talked the whole way in the car. We moved off of depressing conversation and talked about her school, my job and other things. Leah and Edward were both calm which made for an easy drive. We were excited, counting mile markers as we went, each one we passed was another mile closer to sanctuary.

I should have known.

Good things don't last very long. When I calculated we'd be there by dinner, that's when it happened.

The car sputtered and jerked as it used the last bit of gas. I let it coast as if that final fifty feet would make a difference. My car had served me well and it was time to leave it behind.

We were seventy-four miles away.

We had three weeks before they closed their gates. I was certain we would make it.

With the red Radio Flyer wagon loaded with supplies, Hannah, Edward and I began the remainder of the journey on foot.

15

WITHOUT SIGHT

When I mentally planned my family's exodus to sanctuary, I truly believed I'd thought of everything. From clothing to food, the red wagon for walking and carrying our things. What I didn't think about was the actual walking.

I debated on whether to stay on the highway. Even though it was a clear shot, there was nowhere to hide if needed.

Hannah's knowledge of the area only extended about thirty miles beyond Sissonville, WV, after that she was done.

We ran out of gas just outside of Huntington, and looking at the map, we were beyond all the marked safe zones. Our best bet was to follow the Ohio River for a few miles, then cut back up to be near the road.

It was easier said than done.

I didn't take into account that the wagon wouldn't move all that great if we weren't on a smooth surface, or the weather. I never planned on the weather. Autumn had set in early, the air was chilled and an overcast sky didn't help. I also didn't think about my injuries. I had been beaten so badly it hurt with every move I made.

The walking did seem to keep Edward calm. Leah followed us from the car down to the river, but with each step we took, she lagged further behind. That was until we paused then she'd catch up again.

"Should we find a sidewalk or something?" Hannah asked, as she stopped and picked up a bottle of water that fell from the wagon.

"We will, just a little further."

"Do you know this town?"

"No. I'm looking at the map."

"Too bad there's no internet. Could do that earth thing and see what it looks like."

"It would be nice." It wasn't that far to the river or to the town of Huntington, I kept trudging along. Edward to my chest and Hannah picking up the items that flew about whenever I hit a bump.

"I don't get it," I said.

"Get what?"

"Where is everyone? I mean, this virus or whatever it is couldn't have killed everyone or turned them into those things."

"Yes, it could have," she said. "You should have seen Morgantown. One day it was fine, the next day the whole city was hit. We

131

survived because my dad had us in the basement, sealed in. We weren't exposed to it."

"Okay, I understand that, but even though it seems like a lifetime, it wasn't that long ago that we found out about sanctuary happening and our area was scheduled for fire bombing."

"It was long enough that people left. When we did, there were a ton of people leaving. Roads got jammed fast."

"Wait. Wait." I waved my hand about to stop her. "I am really confused. Your parents have been gone for a month. They just told us a couple days ago about Sanctuary Sixteen."

She paused in walking and squinted her eyes are me. "Wow. You must have been far away. The radio was reading them off for over a month."

"A month?"

She nodded.

"There was no news, no television."

"There was radio. It wasn't a live person. It was a recording on the emergency thing."

I stomped my foot and groaned. "Oh my God, I figured once the TV went so did everything else."

"Nope."

"No wonder we haven't seen anyone and the gas station lady commented that it was a while since she saw anyone."

"You're behind. How did you find out if you didn't hear it on the radio?"

"We…" I stopped walking and looked down. I didn't expect to see one, not in such a small town. I lifted the paper from the ground. "Flyer. We got one of these. Shit."

"What?"

"This place is getting firebombed in three days. We need to be far away. I don't understand. Usually they clean a place that is overrun with Vee."

"Maybe they all left," she suggested.

"Maybe." I took a few steps then stopped again. "Maybe not."

As we passed the fenced in area of the City Water Company building, I spotted a block ahead with a massive amount of Vee. They were a sea of slow moving bodies and there was no way to get through them.

"Shit."

"What do we do?" she asked.

"Turn around. We need to get out of sight fast."

"That building." She pointed to the Water Company.

"No. Too close. We'll go back. Cross the tracks and get back to the main road. Let's just turn around. If we move quick, they won't catch us."

"There's nowhere to hide up there."

"There's no Vee either." I reached for her arm and we both turned.

Leah was there, she lunged forward, mouth open. Before Hannah could scream, I pushed her out of the way, then shoved Leah.

"Move," I ordered. I clutched Edward tight to me and yanked the wagon.

We moved quickly until we were at a safe distance. Leah was unable to catch us and we made it to the road, out of breath and a few less supplies. Nothing that we wouldn't miss.

Back to where we left off, we continued on the road.

We moved blindly and I felt vulnerable. Even though we could see the road before us, we hadn't a clue what truly waited ahead.

16

COMPANY

Daniel and Jennifer Harvey had a one story, rectangle modular home, two miles outside of Huntington. A line of trees surrounded the property and a fifty foot gravel driveway led to the house. It was a great little house and it looked like Daniel did auto repairs in the large detached garage on the property.

I learned their names because I looked at the mail. I wanted to know who to mentally thank for the refuge that first night. It was the first building we had come to in a while and we had no choice but to stop.

They were a young couple, maybe in their late twenties. Their wedding picture was dated two years earlier. They created a safe haven of their home. Handmade wooden shutters blocked out the windows.

It would have worked had Daniel not left the house and been bitten.

They obviously were fine for a while. I didn't know why he left. It wasn't for food, there were stacks of it on the kitchen counter. Maybe he was getting a car ready.

It was a puzzle mostly easy to piece together when we arrived.

The blood soaked bandages in the bathroom along with ibuprofen in the bedroom told me of a bite and infection.

Bloody handprints decorated the outside of the home, a sign of relentless pounding. The front door was open and a trail of blood and insides led to a fly and maggot fest in the front yard where Jennifer had become one of those 'twitchers' that Hannah talked about.

Half of her face was missing and her head was attached by the neck body, her throat had been ripped apart. Her left shoulder remained along with most of that arm. Beyond that, she was nothing but mush and a few scattered bones. The smell was horrendous, worse than Leah and at first I thought the sight of the flies made the entire thing more sickening, until Jennifer's hand twitched.

Her fingers extended and her one eye moved. Her mouth opened and closed, biting at nothing.

"We can't leave her like that," Hannah said. "We have to do something."

"I will. But let's get you safe inside, okay?" I handed her Edward.

I went in first making sure it was Vee free. It was. Inside the light gray carpet was blood stained and a handgun was on the floor. The coffee table was busted. I could picture what happened. Daniel was bitten, he turned, but wasn't violent. Jennifer probably moved him outside and contemplated on killing him.

Then Daniel got hungry and out of control. She opened the door to shoot him and was overcome. The poor girl fought for her life, probably stumbled out of the house, trying to keep her intestines inside of her when Daniel delivered one last blow.

The house smelled sour, but it was shelter that would do. The door was attached and I could lock it.

I told Hannah to come in, "It doesn't look pretty, but it will work."

When she walked inside, she saw the gun. "You can use that," she said. "To help her out there."

"Um, yeah," I said nervously. "If it's laying here, she probably meant to use it and it's loaded."

"It's a Glock."

I quickly looked at her. "How do you know?"

"It's says it on the handle. You don't know guns, do you?"

"Not really." I reached for it.

"Careful picking it up. There's no safety and it probably has a round in the chamber. Really all you need. Just go out there and use the one ready."

"You make it sound easy. Like you fired a gun before."

"I have."

"You're eleven."

"More like twelve," she argued. "Not very good. Only been shooting a year. Mostly rifles for hunting. My father made me learn all about guns and take that gun safety class."

"Kind of insane to let a kid have a gun."

"Won't be saying that if we're hungry and I bag us a deer. Want me to do it?"

"No!" I snapped. "Absolutely not. No. I got this. Stay." The gun was foreign to my hand and I held it like it was poison. I shut the door and walked out to Jennifer's body.

I didn't want to do it. I had to keep looking at her to feel bad, remorse so I could end what she was going through. What if she knew? What if she had a part of her that remembered?

My hand shook out of control as I aimed, so much so I brought it within a few inches of her head.

I closed my eyes because I just couldn't look at her. Then I fired.

After that I didn't move, not for a few second, then I went back into the house. It was time to settle in for the night.

<>< >< >< >

The sound of the gunshot must have scared Edward because he started fussing and making that horrible newborn scream the moment we closed the door and locked down. I worried, I didn't want to attract Vee or any people, but he was out of control, just like in the barn.

With a wiggle of her fingers, Hannah said, "Give him here. I'll take care of him."

I was grateful and I handed him over. She took him in a back bedroom to feed and change him while I double checked the doors and windows and brought in the red wagon. The place would have been nice, but it was a mess. Using bed sheets, I covered the blood in the living room and sprinkled carpet deodorizer around for the smell. My wounds needed attention and there was plenty of water in the house to clean up. I wanted a good night's sleep and looked forward to it. Both Hannah and I were exhausted and I felt safe in the house.

We didn't need to touch our supplies. I found a can of beef stew in the cupboard and fixed that with crackers.

"You aren't taking their stuff, are you?" Hannah asked. "We have enough. You should leave it for the next people."

"I'm not taking it. And there won't be next people."

"How do you know?"

"I do." I set the bowl in front of her and lifted Edward from her arms.

"You ain't leaving that, are you?"

I wondered what she was talking about and then I saw she looked at the gun on the counter by the refrigerator.

"No, I just don't need it right now." I sat down and sighed out in pain. It took stopping to show me how horrible I felt.

"You okay?"

"I'll get there. Eat."

"We should stay here a couple days. Let you heal."

"I'll be fine. Besides, they're wiping out this town soon and this house is too close to it."

"And the longer we stay, the more chance Leah will find us."

"Unless she was following and we didn't see, she's gone."

"That make you sad?" she asked.

"A little. I wish I was hungry though." I lifted the spoon, brought some to my mouth, but didn't feel like eating it. I replaced the spoon in the bowl and looked down to Edward. He cuddled up against me. "Boy, I have to tell you, Hannah, you have the magic touch with him."

"I know what I'm doing. I was waiting another year and I was gonna be the best babysitter around. I was just eight when my sister was born and my mom used to let me feed her 'cause she'd eat for me. Mom said it takes patience to feed a baby right and know what it wants."

"You have that. I just wasn't ready for it."

"I'll help as much as I can. He's quiet now."

"Just let me know if you don't feel like it. I don't want you to get tired of helping me with him. He's not your responsibility."

"It's okay. I don't mind." She lifted the spoon to her mouth, shoveled a heap into her mouth and then another.

"You must be really…" I paused when I noticed the white bandage on her forearm. "What happened to your arm?"

"Nothing. I got scratched on the barn door."

"Were you bit?"

"No!" she answered quickly. "It was dark, I got cut on the barn door. Honest."

"Hannah, if you're bit, you need to tell me."

"I ain't bit or scratched. Okay?" She shook her head. "If I was you'd know soon enough anyhow. But I'm not. If you wanna see, I'll show you."

"No. That's fine."

"See?" she pulled the bandage exposing a gash.

"It doesn't look infected, that's a good thing."

"Because I didn't wash it in the creek," she said seriously then smiled. She finished off her bowl. "Is there more?"

"Take mine. I'm not really hungry." I pushed my bowl to her. She put it inside her empty one. "If you want—"

We both jumped when there was a pounding at the door.

"Hey! Open up! Help!" the male voice shouted. "I know someone's in there. I see the light."

My eyes widened. What light? I knew we had lanterns but the shutters were closed. I stood up and looked around. "How does he know? All the windows are sealed and the door…" I cringed. Daniel and Jennifer sealed the house for safety, not to block out the light and they never covered the tiny window on the front door.

"You letting him in?" Hannah asked.

"Please help us. There's these things out here and…"

I heard the scream coming from outside. A bloodcurdling scream.

"Help!" The man pounded harder.

I handed Edward to Hannah. "Take him in the back room, lock the door."

"But…"

"Go." I walked to the living room and reached for the door. After undoing the lock, I barely opened it and the man barged in.

He slammed the door shut with his body, then hurried and locked it. I could hear a Vee, trying to get in. The stranger leaned forward to the door, head against it. His dirty and longer dark hair dangled in his face. "Thanks."

"Are you okay?" I asked.

He nodded. "They got my friend."

"I'm sorry. How many are out there? It doesn't sound like much."

"Five. Four. I don't know."

I stepped back when he spoke and I caught a good whiff of him. He was a mixture of odors that I didn't want to imagine what they were. "Why are you out there at night?"

"Because there's very little shelter out there on this stretch of road or haven't you noticed?" He breathed heavily and turned around, removing the hair for his face. "Not expecting company, I see."

"What?"

It was odd and he chuckled, swinging his hand around, pointing at the sheets.

"This isn't my house. This was all there was."

"I hear you brother." He extended his hand. "Curt."

I apprehensively shook it. "Calvin."

"Cal. I smell food. Tell me you have food. I have eaten in two days."

"Yeah, I do. This way."

"Sorry if I track up your carpet, I stepped on something out there."

Jennifer's remains were what came to my mind. I led him to the kitchen. I wanted to get to know him, gauge him before I let Hannah and the baby out. There was something off about him. Then again it could have been my imagination.

"Looks like I'm just in time for supper." He sat down in Hannah's seat.

"Go on. I'm not hungry. Eat." I sat as well. "You headed to Sanctuary Sixteen?"

"From." He answered. "Water? Do you have water?"

"Um sure." I stood and grabbed a bottle from the counter. "You were at Sixteen?"

"Yep. I left. Not for me. Everywhere are tents. Living with people you don't know. Soldiers with guns everywhere.'

"Aren't they there to keep people safe?"

"Yeah, but it feels like a prison. What happened to you?"

"I was jumped."

He raised his eyebrows. "Happens all the time down there. That's why I wanted out. They take your stuff when you get there. Community share thing. Problem was, when I left, things were picked clean. You got supplies?"

"Some."

"I spotted the wagon in the living room. You have more than some."

He raised an eyebrow as he hoovered the food. There was something creepy about his look.

"There's plenty here in this house. So you can take what you need."

"I'll do that. Not much out there. I'm gonna take all I can. I have to plan for the future."

"You didn't mention where you're headed," I said.

"You alone?" he asked without answering me.

"Yes."

Just then Edward made some noise.

Curt's head shot to the left and he stood. "Doesn't sound like alone. Man, you are full of untruths." He stood.

"Look," I told him. "It's my family. I don't know why you're here or what you want."

"Are you kidding me? I was pounding on the door for help. If you would have answered, my friend would still be alive."

"I did answer. You have to understand, I'm being cautious. I have to be."

"Because you can't take care of yourself," he said. "That's obvious. I'm surprised you still have stuff. And you're being awful nervous."

"Wouldn't you be?"

He laughed and tried to get past me.

"Where are you going?"

"Think I want to meet the family."

"Leave them be. You can go or stay. Take the supplies you want, but just don't worry about them. I don't understand why this is important to you?"

"Because I want to know who I'm tossing out in the middle of the night to die. I'm like that, you know."

"What? You're insane. We're going nowhere."

He laughed. "You think you're gonna stop me from throwing you out? You would have already. Look at you, you're in no condition to… *throw* me out. You haven't a clue how to survive in this hell world or else you would have had that gun in your hand when you opened the door."

I just stared.

"By the way, where is that gun? The one that was on the living room floor? Man, we should have grabbed that. But I thought, who the hell would be coming here? My mistake. Or maybe it's still there under the sheets." He tipped his chin arrogantly as he stepped to me. "Yeah, we were here first. This morning actually. Left for more supplies. That can of stew… was probably mine." He winked then shoved easily by me and headed to the hallway.

"Hey!" I shouted.

"I am going to be nice. Let you leave on your own. That way no one gets hurt by me and I have a clean conscious." He whistled short and loud. "Calvin's family? Time to go." At the end of the narrow hall, Curt opened the door to this right, then after looking inside, he opened the next door exposing Hannah sitting on the bed. Edward was covered completely in her arms with a blanket. Curt burst into laughter. "Well, well, well. What do we have? You certainly have your hands full, Calvin. A baby and a little girl. Tell you what, I'll help you out. You take the baby, leave the girl. Kinda gets lonely at night around…"

Fueled with disgust and anger, I charged at Curt slamming my body into him, we hit against the door frame and I slugged my fist into his gut.

He grunted once, grabbed me, spun me around and slammed me into the wall.

"Well look who has balls after all." He held me firmly by the scruff of my shirt. The next thing I knew I had a gun under my chin. "I was going to let you go. Now I'm not."

"Leave her be. She's just a kid."

"Why you think I got kicked out of Sanctuary? Huh?"

A single gunshot rang out and Curt's eyes widened, his grip on me loosened. His face had a look of shock just before he dropped sideways to the floor

He had been shot in the hip. Groaning he rolled to his back and tried to reach for his weapon which fell from his hand.

Hannah, with a cold expression stepped out of the bedroom, gun extended and focused on Curt.

"Hannah! No!" I shouted. Hannah didn't heed my warning. She fired a single shot to his chest.

He wasn't dead.

I was in shock at what I saw, how Hannah could have done what she did, so calm and without hesitation. She lowered her aim and stared.

"Hannah, are you okay?"

She spoke dazed. "I couldn't let him take me or hurt you. I couldn't." She nudged him with her foot and Curt coughed, grabbing his chest wound. "What do we do with him, Cal?"

Curt coughed. "Help."

I literally scoffed, maybe even laughed at the absurdity of his request.

After thinking about it, I raced into the living room and peeked out the shutter.

I could only see two Vee and they were hovered over a body. I returned to the hall. "Okay they're busy out there. We can do this. Grab an arm and help me move him."

The task wasn't quite as simple as I hoped it would be. A battered guy and a twelve-year-old girl, dragging a man across the small home. He wasn't big, but he gave his all in struggling as we pulled his arms.

He coughed and choked, blood shot from his mouth. He even pleaded for his life. As if we would change our minds and suddenly have a change of heart. He may have been bleeding and breathing, but in a sense, he was already dead. I was just making sure he got what he deserved. If he came after us, threatened me, made sick suggestions about Hannah and did all that with ease, then he had done it before.

That was my justification for opening the door and rolling him out.

He screamed for a while, longer than his friend. He must have felt every finger nail dig into him, every bite as it tore flesh from him.

I stood there for a little while listening, processing all that happened. Fighting the guilt that tried to creep up. Eventually, he went silent and I walked away from the door. I still don't know what happened first, if he stopped screaming or I simply stopped listening and caring.

17

DANGLE

September 6

It would be a late start to the day, but I was fine with that. Both Hannah and I were well rested. I slept so soundly on the reclining chair with Edward on my chest, I was afraid I rolled over on him. I hadn't moved. My body was stiff and sore, but I had a clear head.

Daniel and Jennifer had coffee and the propane tank was still full. I was able to light the stove and boil water, run it through the filter and make a pot. It tasted good and I found a huge thermos, filling that for the road trip. That was my prize find. Hannah's was a hair brush and hair bands. She brushed her hair for a good fifteen minutes, then struggled with the ponytail.

I had just finished packing everything to leave when she game into the kitchen pretty frustrated. "You don't by chance know how to do a braid, do you? Guess not." She turned.

"I do."

She stopped. "Really? You ain't fooling me are you?"

"Nope." I pulled out a chair. "Sit."

"How do you know how? You're a man."

"I was a married man and I had a sister. I know braids. Don't tell anyone."

"Seems silly you would say that. Who am I gonna tell?"

"You never know." After she sat down, I started braiding her hair.

"Is your sister alive?"

"I like to think so. She lived in Germany with her husband. In fact, I'll believe she is."

"How old are you, Calvin?"

"Thirty-seven."

"Thirty-seven and you haven't fired a gun?"

"Not everyone shoots guns, Hannah." I worked the braid. "I wasn't much of an outdoor kind of guy. My job had me sitting behind a desk."

"That's sounds boring."

"Not really. I liked math."

"Oh, now I know you're strange."

I laughed and added the band to the end of her braided ponytail. "There. Done."

"That was fast." She reached back and felt. "It feels nice."

"I'm good. Now, are you ready to leave? It's almost noon."

"You look to see if there were any out there?" she asked.

"Last I looked, I didn't see any. Let's go before they come."

"I'm ready. Let me run and pee and steal that toilet paper so we have it for the road."

"You do that."

She started to leave the kitchen and paused. "You look better today."

"Thanks, I feel better."

Hannah darted off and I gathered the remaining items, placing and securing them in the wagon. Edward was on the chair and I put him in the carrier and then moved the wagon near the door. I dreaded pulling it down the four steps.

"Hannah, you alright?"

"Yeah, I'm just getting something," she replied, then I heard her feet slamming against the floor as she ran my way. "Ready. I was getting some stuff."

I noticed how much fatter that Barbie backpack was as she slung it over her shoulder. "What the heck? How many rolls of toilet paper did you take?"

"I took stuff, that's all."

I shook my head and opened the door. When I did, Hannah giggled.

"Well, ain't that just true love," she said.

Sarcastic as her comment was, I knew what she meant.

Leah had found us. I don't know if she knew, or stopped because of the Curt and friend buffet in the yard. But she dropped a severed arm and tilted her head when she saw us.

I waited a moment, thinking Leah was going to attack, but she didn't. So with Hannah's help, we lowered the wagon to the ground and we were on our way.

It was a good day for walking. The weather cooperated. It wasn't too hot or too cold, in fact it was perfect. There were a lot of hills and slopes to climb, I wondered how Hannah talked so much and didn't lose her breath.

For the first twenty minutes she wouldn't shut up about how Curt was a twitcher and how I just left him there.

My attitude was, "oh well," because after thinking about it all night, I was out of sympathetic feelings.

Leah followed. She lagged behind farther and farther until we stopped for a break and then she caught up.

"I want to do about ten miles today," I said. "Maybe more before we stop for the night. Somewhere around Windsor Falls, I want to start looking for a place to stay."

Hannah didn't reply.

"Are you listening to me?" I glanced over to her and saw she kept looking back at Leah. "Are you worried she's gonna attack?"

"No, she's good for a while. She ate on Curt. I'm just... she keeps coming. Keeps following like a puppy dog. So sad. Or like Torina."

"Okay, I'll bite. Who is Torina?"

"When I was in the second grade, there was a new girl named Torina. She didn't speak English very well. It was odd because not many people in West Virginia don't speak English. I was nice to her and she kept following me and following me."

"Until you stopped and played with her?"

"No. I couldn't. I didn't understand her. How was I supposed to be friends if I didn't understand a word she said? Anyhow, you think she knows?"

"Torina?"

"No, silly, Leah," Hannah said. "You think she knows you?"

"I think it's possible. I mean, if a piece of the brain is functioning enough to move the body, maybe a tiny piece remembers. Or at least I like to think she remembers me instead of looking at me like a McDonald's menu."

"If you think she remembers you, then that it isn't right what you're doing."

"You mean not putting her down?" I asked.

"No, letting her walk around like that. Calvin, she's naked from the waist down."

"I know she's naked from the waist down, she died after giving birth."

"It's your wife. Don't you care that people see her like that?"

I stopped for a second. "Are you serious?"

"I mean, what would she say if she knew you let her walk around all exposed? I know I'd be mad. I feel bad for her."

Shaking my head, I walked again. "Hannah, what do you want me to do?"

"Put some clothes on her."

I laughed. "Yeah, right away. I'll just stop, walk up to her, ask her to sit down while I put a pair of pants on her."

"Now's the time. She just had Curt so she'll be calm. She won't try to bite you."

"Hannah…"

"It don't need to be pants. It can be a dress. Nothing fancy. Be easy to put on her. Toss it over her head. We can find one of those dresses like my grandma used to wear to cover her big boobs and belly. Big old flowery thing that floats in the wind and shows her legs. Anything. We'll find something. But for goodness sakes, Calvin, cover up her womanhood."

I believe I actually snorted a laugh at that remark. "Womanhood? Okay, if we see one of those big old flowery things that float in the wind, I'll put it on her."

"Do it before she's hungry again."

"I can't believe how much this is bothering you."

"It does," she replied. "'Cause I'm a girl. Girls are private about those things. You don't think about it because boys aren't private. I mean they just whip it out to piss on a tree. No shame."

"Oh my God."

"And it's sad, Calvin, it's just really sad. Look at her."

"I did."

"She keeps on trudging. And every time I look, things keep fallin' out of her lady parts…"

"Jesus, Hannah." I stopped and brought my hand to my face.

"What? They do. What do you suppose it is?"

"I don't know and… can we… not talk about things falling out of her lady parts."

"Okay. I just thought you'd want to know."

"Thank you for that."

"Come to think about it. Pants wouldn't be all that good. You wouldn't want to be putting them on her when she releases…"

"Hannah!" I barked her name. "Please. Just… talk about something else."

"Okay." She went silent for a few seconds as we walked, then she started rambling on again about Curt.

A part of me wondered if things did bother her and her lackadaisical manner of talking about them, was her own therapy.

There was a lot about Hannah I still had to learn. One thing I was sure of, she liked to talk… a lot. Even though she made me cringe and drove me a little nuts at times, for the most part, I was glad she was taking the journey with me.

18

TRIPLE M

The shortest distance between two points was indeed a straight line, one that we could have taken. However, since cutting through trees and over farms was not an option with the wagon we stayed on the paved road.

Avoiding the main highway, we took secondary roads that the map showed ran perpendicular to the highway. The black top was a lot easier on our feet. Eventually it would cross the interstate, however, we could pick it up again.

There were more options for shelter plus we didn't see another soul.

People were as dangerous as the Vee.

"You think people live in some of these places, still?" Hannah asked. "I mean it's way out here. No sick people. There were cows back there, did you see?'

"I did. When you picked those apples."

"They were ripe. Falling from the tree. I had to. Didn't want them to go to waste. Want one?" She held it up for me.

"After being beat up, my teeth couldn't bite into that."

"Want me to cut it for you? I have a knife. Sharp one, too."

"No, and why do you have a knife."

"Just in case."

"That doesn't surprise me. I don't know why I asked. Are you're sure you're only ten?"

"You do that on purpose. You know I'm gonna be twelve."

"You just act and look older."

"I may look older. That's because I'm the tallest kid in my grade, but you only think I act older because you don't know kids too good."

"That's true. For what it's worth, I think you're very brave for all you've been through and doing it on your own."

"I'm not on my own."

"Before."

"I didn't want to be alone. Just didn't have a choice," she said. "Why you being all nice to me?"

"I'm making conversation and I'm always nice to you."

She snickered. "I can talk about Curt."

"No."

"I could talk about how we walked a hundred miles and you still ain't got pants on Leah."

"We only walked ten. Start looking for a place."

"That's why I asked that question about people still living in their houses. Maybe people are home and we can't just go in their houses."

"Then we'll walk."

"There's a house up there." She pointed.

I looked. In the distance, back from the road was a yellow two-story house. I thought I spotted a fence but I wasn't sure.

"They have a stable. Maybe they have a horse," Hannah said.

"Are you going to tell me you ride, too?"

"Don't everyone."

"No, but that's one thing I do know, I know horses."

"You ride?" she asked.

"No, did I say I ride? I said I know them. From the track. I used to bet on them."

"For a guy who likes math, you're really funny."

"I did used to tell good jokes."

"Oh, tell me one."

"Okay, let me think." I walked, trying my hardest to recollect a good joke she would understand. "Alright, I have one. Why did the…" I paused when I saw them. My voice dropped. "Expired Vee?"

"I think something is missing there, Calvin. Why did the expired Vee, what?"

"No." I shook my head. "Expired Vee in the middle of the road."

"Why are there expired Vee in the middle of the road?"

"Yeah."

"Um, because they couldn't get to the other side?"

"Huh?"

"Your joke, is that the punchline? 'Cause Cal, it ain't very funny. Might be too soon to tell Vee jokes."

"No. No. It's not a joke. Up there." I showed her. "Four of them."

"You think they're them?"

"Yeah, I do."

"How can you tell from this far?"

"Their position."

It was hard to explain to her what I meant. When I was Hannah's age, the house four doors down caught on fire. Four people lived in the house and I watched it, like everyone else, as it burned to the ground despite the best efforts of the fire department. When it was done and

162

the flames put out, they sorted through the rubble and uncovered the bodies.

Their arms and legs were bent up and inward as if the muscles retracted, hands slightly reaching, fingers bent. Their mouths wide open, probably from gasping for their last bit of air. Like the ash people in the photos from Pompeii. Burned, yet frozen in that pose.

The man in the beer distributor had that pose. Even at a distance, I could see the four on the road did as well.

Only they weren't burnt.

When I neared them, I examined each one visually, their skin had pruned and even outside, there were very little flies.

"What happened to them?" Hannah asked.

"They just dropped. Expired as I call it."

"None of them shot?"

"Nope. Doesn't look like it, and they weren't bitten."

"So these are the ones that just caught it by the air."

I shook my head. "Can't be sure. You know a bite or scratch isn't the only way. You can get their spit in your eyes or mouth or, well, other ways."

"Sex."

"Hannah!"

"I heard the news," she said. "They told us not to have sex with an infected person. I don't get why someone would want to do that. Wouldn't they be afraid the Vee would take a bite out of them?"

"I don't think that's what they meant. I think they meant having relations before the person turned but was infected."

"Maybe you're right. Maybe expire is the best word for it. Maybe the ones that got it from the air are the most violent, but the ones that expire and end. Like this apple that fell from the tree. Pretty soon it would expire and shrivel up too."

"Wow, that's pretty prolific and smart."

"Thanks."

"And that might be it. Hopefully."

"If they expire it could end."

"Yeah, it could." I took another look at the three women and a man on the ground in the ash people position, then we moved around them and headed for the yellow house.

The winding road created an optical illusion and the house didn't sit that far back. About ten feet from the pavement was a short fence, more for decoration.

"I don't think this is keeping any of those things out," Hannah said. "You suppose they thought it would?"

"I don't think that was its purpose." I stared at the house.

"Ain't much protection from the Vee. They would just bump into it and fall right over. Can't be more than three feet. Think someone is in there? I do, I hear chickens."

"Well, if they're not, we're having chicken for dinner."

Hannah laughed.

"What's so funny?"

"Like you're gonna catch a chicken and kill it?"

"I guess you have?"

"Not me, those things are fast. Ever see the movie Rocky?"

"Yes," I smiled and grabbed the gate. "Let's go find out."

"What about her?" Leah pointed back to Leah.

"She's still at a distance. Let's go knock on the door." I pulled the gate.

The front door flung open. "Stop!" a woman hollered. "Don't move. Don't move an inch."

I raised my arms. "We don't mean trouble. Please don't shoot."

"I'm not going to shoot," she said. "Just don't step forward. I don't want you to blow up. I booby trapped the whole front."

I looked to Hannah and carefully stepped back. "Booby trapped? What is it with you southern women?"

"We take care of ourselves," Hannah replied.

"Yeah you do." I peered up when I heard the slam of the screen door. The woman stood there wearing a blue flowered housecoat. A rounder woman, with brass blonde hair that was kind of poofy. She was mature, maybe in her late fifties, early sixties.

"Look, Calvin." Hannah whispered. "She's wearing one of those dresses. Ask her for one."

"Shh."

"She looks just like my grandma."

The woman moved her arm about. "Move to the edge of the fence by the tree. There will be another gate. I'll walk you through the yard so you don't hit a trip wire," she said, stepping off the porch.

I lifted my hand in a wave and we headed towards the tree.

"Ma'am," I said. "I hate to bother you. We didn't know if the house was empty or not. We have our own supplies…"

"I see that." She nodded her head at the wagon. "That a baby?" she asked.

"It is. My son." I cringed when Edward made a little whimper. "We need to stop for the night and rest, we'll be gone first light. We can even stay in your barn over there. He won't make much noise."

"Oh, that won't be necessary." She opened the gate. "Come in."

"Thank you, we…" I stopped talking when Hannah, just walked up to the woman and wrapped her arms around her waist. She closed her eyes and smiled as she pressed her head against her. "Hannah."

"Oh, she is just like my grandma," Hannah gushed. "So soft. I miss my grandma."

"Hannah, let the lady go."

"Just a few more seconds, Calvin."

"Hannah."

"Oh, pumpkin." She returned the embrace to Hannah. "Any time you need a hug, I will give you one. Okay?"

Hannah nodded and stepped back. "I like your dress."

"Thank you. I don't usually run around in one. I just hung the wash out back to…" She pointed to the street. "She with you?"

I looked and sure enough Leah drew close. I was surprised the woman wasn't shocked or scared.

"Yes, sort of. She tags along. She…. she is… was my wife."

Seemingly unfazed, the woman nodded, shut the gate and led us to her home.

She introduced herself as Mama Mavis Martin, but we could call her Mama, or Mavis. Everyone always did. For as long as she could remember she was the town mother. Everyone ran to her. That made sense.

It was a mad mixture of things all wrapped up in a surreal package. A picture-perfect small farm, booby trapped perimeters, a body double for Hannah's grandmother, a kitchen that smelled of cinnamon, complete with a Vee husband named George whom she kept in the fenced in turnaround area by the stable. All of which was present by a woman rocking a house dress serving up apple pie as if we were the new neighbors coming to visit.

The pie was amazing.

Hannah loved it and dumped those apples she picked right on the table. "Take them if you can use them," she said. "I won't eat them all before they spoil."

"You sure?" she asked. "How about I make you something before you leave? Something you can take with you that won't spoil too fast."

"Okay," Hannah said excitedly.

Mavis' attention was drawn to me when Edward stated to fuss.

"Have you been traveling with the baby long?" she asked.

"Since he was born. That's only been a couple days."

"I have a basinet upstairs in the small bedroom. You can put him down. Maybe that's what he needs. Babies tend to get sore when handled too much. I bet his skin is especially tender. Why don't you lay him down?"

"That might be a good idea. Thank you."

"I can show you…"

"No. I'll go. I'll find it. Be right back."

I left the kitchen. I think I needed to see the house, learn the woman. Who was she? Why was she being so nice? I wondered if it was all a set up for something bad, or she was insane?

The bedroom with the bassinet was easy to find. It was at the top of the stairs to the right. I placed Edward in the basinet. He didn't seem to like it much. He fussed and screamed, his little arms flailing about. His perfect little face, with tiny features, just looked so angry. Like he was pissed at the world. I wanted him to calm down. I needed a break and I was sure Hannah did too.

Thinking maybe if I let him be, he'd go to sleep, I turned to leave the room and Hannah was there. I jumped.

"You scared me."

"Sorry. You left his binky downstairs. That'll calm him." She rushed by me to the bassinette and leaned over. "Hey there little guy. Here you go."

He let out a few short screams, fighting any satisfaction he may get from the pacifier. Then he finally gave in. He was quiet except for the sucking noise.

"There. All better," Hannah said with a smile.

"Hannah, I don't know what I'd do without you."

"Have a really loud and fussy baby all the time, that's for sure. Come on, Calvin. Mama Mavis is making tea."

I stepped out of her way as she dashed by me. "Okay then." After taking another peek at Edward, I went downstairs.

In my pass through the living room, I paused at the sofa table and looked at all the photographs that were set out. The photos spanned her entire life. From a young hot wife to the loveable looking woman she had become. She had children, lots of them. Five from what I counted. Many grandchildren, too. It made me sad to think of her losses.

Hearing the clanking of cups and the chattering between her and Hannah, I realized the way to get to know her wasn't just by the photographs, but by talking to her as well.

Tea sounded good and I joined them in the kitchen.

Mama Mavis was a wonderful woman, at least to us. She missed her family dearly and was definitely a 'Pleasantville' version of an apocalypse survivor.

She cooked a wonderful stew, fresh applesauce and biscuits. I was happy with the pie, we arrived so late, the dinner was a welcome surprise.

I had washed up and she gave me a clean shirt and jeans and I thanked her for them. "Best I felt in days."

"You don't look it," Mavis said. "Here." She rattled a brown pill bottle and placed it in front of me. "Antibiotics. Take them. The whole bottle. They'll help. You don't have far to go to Sanctuary City, they won't let you in if you're sick. Right now, you just took a beating, couple days you'll look better."

"Thank you again." I clutched the bottle.

"Supper's on the table, Hannah. Come eat,' Mavis said.

Hannah stared out the backdoor. "George is chasing something out there."

"Probably a mouse. We have many back there. He'll get one," Mavis said. "Then he'll calm down. It doesn't take much to calm them down. Few bites. They really don't ingest it. They just chew. I guess it seems kinda sadistic to keep them. Because he was my husband I couldn't do it. I couldn't kill him"

"Calvin is gonna shoot his wife in the head first chance he feels ready for it."

"Oh stop. I did not say that," I said.

"What happened to him?" Hannah asked. "How did George get like that?"

"He got bit," Mavis responded. "Was helping a neighbor down the road. Trying to pack them up and get them going. Their boy was sick. He bit him. George turned within a couple days. I guess I'm just waiting for the good Lord to take him."

"I see you have a stable. Did you have horses?" I asked.

"At one time. I don't anymore."

"Did George eat them?" Hannah asked.

"Hannah!" I scolded.

Mavis smiled and shook her head. "No. That would be way too much for George to eat, now wouldn't it. No. I bartered them. A man named Jason came up with the idea to start a transportation service from different places in the area to Sanctuary Sixteen and Thirteen. They pay him with stuff and he takes them. I bartered for goods in our deal, I gave him the horses and cart and made a nice deal with him for what people paid him. He's a good man. Stays true to his word. Drops off supplies on his way there every single trip. Usually him and his traveling folks spend the night. Then they go on their way. He's been doing it for several weeks now. He's about due. Takes a different road back up north and this one down."

Hannah gushed with excitement. "Oh, Mama Mavis, we would've met anyhow. I was waiting on the next transport. He was taking a while."

"Sometimes he hangs out at the sanctuary to rest up. Plus it's been raining a lot."

Hannah asked, "What's it like? Do you know? Did Jason tell you? What's Sanctuary City like?"

"Well, little one, they're safe there. He said they're like tent cities. He said sometimes they get kind of rough. They clean the rift raff out of there. Get rid of the rowsers pretty fast, I hear.

"Did you ever think to go with him?" I inquired.

"No, heavens no." Mavis shook her head. "Have you looked around my place? I have it made. My own water, garden, food supply, and even if the bartering doesn't last, I have enough. It's safe from those things. Very few come up this way. That hill is a trudge."

"Then why the explosives?" I asked.

"Amongst other things I spent seventeen years in the service back in my heyday. I'm pretty good." She winked. "The traps aren't for the infected, they're for the people that try to get my stuff. I know when they're coming. I have battery operated sensors out on the road. Been hit enough. Jason taught me those lessons. Gotta love that man."

Hannah paused in eating, then a dreamy look came over her. "You're so pretty and smart. Just like my grandma."

Mavis sighed out with an 'ah,' laying her hand on Hannah's face. "You are welcome to stay here. You know that?" Then she looked at me. "You as well. I can use the help with the wood during the winter."

"Wow, thank you. I'll think about it. Part of me wants to make it to sanctuary. Like a goal, but if the invitation will stay open."

"Absolutely," she said.

"Hannah," I said. "If you want to stay…"

"Not without you, Calvin," she said. "You need me. You saved me."

"What?" I laughed.

"Calvin's a hero?" Mavis questioned.

"Yep." Hannah nodded.

"Oh, I am not a hero. Never was and probably never will be. I don't have it in me. I'm an accountant. Besides, you…" I pointed my fork at her. "You saved me. You saved Edward."

"That's how you saved me," Hannah said. "Them men, they weren't nice men. Not at all. They were at Pastor Jim's. Pastor Jim sent me with them to Mr. Mills." Then oddly, she grew sad and spoke in a serious way like I hadn't heard her do. "The night with you and Edward. Two of them had me. Said they wanted to have fun. Then Edward kept fussing." She looked at Mavis. "He was doing that scream thing he does. Over and over. The men stopped 'cause they said they wanted to go get him. Kill him. Crush his skull. Kill Calvin. They left me and I followed. They didn't touch me. So you see, Calvin, you being there saved me."

Mavis laid her hand on Hannah's. "I'm sorry you had to go through that."

"That's the way it is, right?" She shrugged. "It was tried before so I went to Mr. Mills. Always was told to go to an adult. Well, he just said, 'Girl, deal with it, you wanna live here, live anywhere, you'll do what it takes.' When them men got me, I guess I thought I had to do what it takes."

At that instant, I got sick. I jumped up with an "excuse me" and darted out the door, trying my hardest not to get sick. I grabbed the back porch railing, trying to catch my breath, stop the gagging. Then when I spotted George eating that mouse, I lost it.

Every bit of my stew left my body. My stomach wretched. I was so focused on getting to sanctuary, my survival, Edward's, even Leah's, I never paid attention to what was happening in the world around me. That poor girl lost everyone and still was getting hit hard. It sickened me, physically sickened me.

I got my bearings and went back into the house.

"You alright?" Mavis asked.

"You okay, Calvin?"

I nodded and crouched down before Hannah. "I am so sorry for everything you have gone through. Everything. I can't do anything about what happened, but I can about what's gonna happen. You are a kid, Hannah. A kid and you should *never* have to do what it takes, not in this world, not in any world. As long as you are with me, you'll be a kid, never more than a kid and I'll try my damndest to make sure you never have to do… what it takes. Got that?"

She nodded a couple times and wrapped her arms around my neck.

I had seen Hannah as a child, but sadly it never registered. It would from now on. I made a promise to myself. I may not have been the strongest man or the bravest, but I would do what I could to protect Hannah as much as I did my son. They were our future. Not me, not Mavis and not those things out there… the children were.

Unfortunately, there weren't many left.

19

À LA CARTE

September 7

Hannah's twelfth birthday was not forgotten. Not by me and not by Mavis. She made her some applesauce to go, and we sang 'Happy Birthday' over a pancake. Hannah was thrilled, her eyes lit up and she smiled.

Mavis also gave Hannah a necklace of fake pearls and just because she wanted it so badly, and since Leah was calm, I put one of Mavis' house dresses on her.

We were packed up and ready to go and I actually felt bad taking Hannah. It was a good place, a safe place for her. Mavis was a motherly type that would take good care of her. Hannah insisted she didn't want to stay without me.

"If I don't go with you, who's gonna feed Edward?" Hannah asked.

"Me," I replied.

"No offense, but I don't think you do it right. He always eats for me and gets quiet."

"I guess he does."

"Mama Mavis said we can come back. If Sanctuary City sucks, can we do that?"

"Yes, without a doubt we will do that."

We hugged Mavis goodbye and took that back road that would cross the highway. I knew once we crossed that highway, we'd stop again and be even closer to Sanctuary City Sixteen. I couldn't figure out why Hannah wanted to stay with me, why she picked walking a beaten path to a tent city instead of staying in a clean and warm farmhouse.

I felt guilty taking her even though she wanted to come. More than likely, she had developed a trust in me.

She was the best company. I felt better, my body was less sore. I had already taken three doses of antibiotics and I swore they were working and making me stronger. Plus, I rested and ate really well.

Hannah commented on how much better I was doing, then she had to comment on Leah.

"Don't she look pretty in that dress?" Hannah asked. "It's big, but she looks pretty. Don't you think?"

Leah didn't look quite as 'pretty' as Hannah said. It had been five days since she had died. When I would see a Vee, to me they all looked the same. With Leah, I noticed everything that was happening to her. She had taken on a greenish appearance, with the exception of her legs, which were purple and black. Sheaths of maggots covered sections of her body. So many that they looked like patches of sheep's fur. Some sort of dark red foam seeped from her nose and mouth and she started moving differently, more rigid.

I thought about Mavis' husband George. How the photos of him in the living room showed a robust man. His clothing was huge on me. Yet, in the turnaround, he was thin, his skin looked more like a leather covering. As if all his body fluid, fat and tissue had left him and all he had was skin covering his bones.

"Calvin?" Hannah called for me. "Don't you think?"

"For her state, yes."

"Bet she was really pretty before all this."

"As a matter of fact, Leah was beautiful," I said.

"What did she do? Did she have a job? Or did she stay home?"

"She was a first grade teacher."

"Oh, then she loved kids, huh?"

I nodded. "She did."

"Was she excited about the baby?"

"I don't think anyone was more excited about this baby than Leah. We really wanted a child. We had a couple babies that just didn't work out and she lost them. So she was thrilled and scared about Edward."

"Did you ever think that might be why she's following you?" Hannah asked. "For the baby?"

"Maybe." I looked back at her. "I think it's just instinct, that's all."

"What's that noise?"

"I'm sorry, what?" My head spun when she changed subjects.

"That noise? Listen."

I stopped walking to hone in.

There were three distinctive sounds. A clicking, a buzzing and a fluttering sound.

It was coming from up ahead of us and I picked up the pace to see what it was.

The entire trip on that back road, up to that point was uneventful. We had walked steadily, stopped periodically, but saw no one. The noise just echoed.

About a quarter mile up the hill and around the bend, we spotted the source of the multiple sounds.

On the side of the road, a horse-drawn cart was tilted in the depression between the road and grassy hillside. A single horse lay on the road, he struggled with the reigns, shaking his head, he tried to get up when he saw us, but his legs gave in and he fell back down.

"Stay back," I told Hannah, and lifted the carrier from my chest and handed Edward to her. "Let me check it out."

"Is the horse alright?"

"I don't know. Stay here."

As I moved closer to the cart, I not only smelled the rotting odor, I heard the buzzing, then I saw the flies. That told me, something had died. Then I saw him, or rather it. The body of a man slumped in a laying position over the driver's bench seat of the cart. If it wasn't for the gray hair, I wouldn't have been able to tell if he were old or young. His body was bloated and purple.

It was a simple cart. One bench and an open area in back. No top on in and the dead man had been exposed to the elements. The horse peered at me as if asking for help.

"What going on, Calvin?" Hannah asked. "Oh no."

I looked, she was right behind me. "I told you to stay back."

"I know you did. I thought I recognized the cart."

"Jason?" I asked.

Hannah nodded.

"This would explain why he was taking so long. He was on his way back. I'm guessing."

"Mavis is gonna be so sad. She really liked Jason. What happened to him?"

Covering my nose and mouth, I stepped closer. "I don't see any injuries. No gunshot wounds. No bites. How old was he? Do you remember?"

"About my grandpa's age."

"He probably had a heart attack. Veered off the road and died."

"That's so sad. He died alone."

"Yeah, it is kind of sad. At least he died peacefully. No Vee have been around. The horse is still here."

"What about the other ones? He had more than one horse."

I took a closer look. I knew horses from the races, but I could only speculate on what had happened. No blood, no carcasses. "The reigns are broke." I showed her the straps. "The others got away. I'm guessing. This one…" I moved closer. The horse jolted. "Easy boy. Easy. His leg is caught up. He couldn't get free. Mavis said it was raining, that's probably the only reason he's still alive."

"How long have they been out here?"

"This happened several days ago. I'm guessing. Looking at…" I pointed at Leah, then at him.

"What are we gonna do? We can't just leave them here."

"No, we won't. First we're gonna help this horse. Untangle him, get him some water. Feed him a couple of those apples you have," I said. "He needs to get his strength back."

"Then what?"

"Then once he's better and strong, we get this cart back on the road."

"With Jason?" she asked.

"No, not with Jason. We move him from the cart."

"You're gonna bury him, right Calvin? You have to bury him. No one gets buried anymore."

"We don't have time to bury him."

"Why not?"

"Why... why not? I don't know. It will take some time to bury him. We're already near stopping time."

"Not like we have an appointment," she said. "You don't like dead people, do you?'

"What?" I nearly laughed in my reaction.

"First you let your wife run about naked and now you wanna toss Jason off to the side of the road, then you have..."

"He's already on the side of the road," I said.

"It just seems disrespectful. He was helping people."

"I hardly call rendering a profit from transporting people helping."

"Calvin. Please."

"Look. We help this horse first. Okay. Life first. Then we will discuss Jason. Fair?" I asked.

"Fair enough," Hannah said.

"Fine. Give me the apples, then just hang back with Edward. Okay. Don't get too close to Leah."

Hannah opened her Barbie pack and handed me an apple before she backed up.

The horse was beautiful, but I could tell he needed help. He wasn't going to just stand right up and trot off anywhere. Not yet.

The situation about Jason the transport man was unfortunate… for him. We had lucked out. That horse and cart would get us to Sanctuary Sixteen and get us there faster. I honestly didn't know how much more Edward could take. He needed to get to sanctuary. He needed medical attention. Finding the horse and cart was a blessing. I was fearful because nothing easy ever is free and something told me, somewhere, somehow, I would have a price to pay.

20

RISE AND SHINE

Once again, my life had become a living example of *Oregon Trail*. My wagon was the cart and the oxen was the one single horse that Hannah named Mary.

Even though Mary wasn't the best gender name for him.

He was a good horse, strong and he devoured the apples. I could tell he had been drinking water that had puddled on the side of the road. It took a good two hours before he was strong enough to stand. That alone was evidence enough why he needed to take it easy. I would walk him, putting only Hannah and the baby in the cart for the first day. I'd pull the wagon because I didn't want to put strain on him. I contemplated going back to Mavis' house and let the horse heal. I felt Edward couldn't afford the delay without medical attention so we kept going.

First thing, as promised, after I got Mary on his feet, I had to tend to Jason. He was still in the cart. His body bloated. Moving him wasn't fun, his skin separated easily and a sticky fluid leaked out.

Thankfully he had a sleeping bag in the cart. I used that to touch him. Every time I bumped him or moved him gasses escaped with a noise adding to the already foul smell, along with bringing out the true child in Hannah. With every noise, she giggled, groaned or made comments.

Somewhere in the process we lost Leah. She wandered off while we tended to Mary and never returned.

"She'll be back," Hannah said. "I bet she went to look for food."

"Well, she had us, usually that's her point of attack first. Remember we're her McDonald's menu?"

"Nah, I think she likes us. She's trained now."

"Hannah, honey, it doesn't work that way," I explained.

"You believe that. When she comes back, you'll see. She'll be all fresh and fed. Maybe she learned to chase mice like George."

"Maybe."

Hannah was right. In my gut, I didn't feel Leah was gone for good either.

So much time had passed in getting the horse and taking care of Jason, we only made it another two miles before making camp for the night.

We found a little league field. Hannah and Edward slept in the dugout. She sprawled across a bench and Edward slept in the basket Mavis had given us.

I was well rested and I stayed up pretty much the whole night, keeping an eye out on things.

I did doze off for a short while, back against the dugout wall. I was confident that I would wake up at the simplest noise. Of course, I was wrong.

"Are you going to Sixteen?" a female voice asked.

I jolted awake.

The sun was behind the tall thin figure of a woman, making her a shadow.

"Is that your horse over there?" she asked.

She stepped closer and I saw her. A woman, maybe a little younger than me. Long dark hair, wearing a dirty tee shirt and jeans. Her face was smeared with dirt.

"If you're going to Sixteen, can I travel with you?"

Before I could answer, Hannah did.

"No."

I looked over my shoulder, Hannah stood there with a scowl on her face.

"Hannah?" I questioned.

"No!" She vigorously shook her head. "We don't know her. I don't want her to come. I don't trust strangers."

The woman held up both her hands. "I understand. My name is Diana. I just don't want to travel the rest of the way alone. I've had problems by myself. I'm sure you guys know the Vee aren't the only bad things."

"We do," I said.

"Judging by your face, I believe you do," Diana said, obviously referencing my healing bruises. "Is that… is that a baby?"

"It's none of your business what I have!" Hannah raced over and covered Edward.

"It's okay." Diana leaned to her right, then took a step. "Hannah? Is that your name? I'll stay away from you. Okay? I know you're scared. I know kids. I have… I have two sons. One is about your age."

"Well, go to them then," Hannah snapped.

Diana lowered her head.

I closed my eyes for a second. "Wow. I've never seen her like this."

"It's alright. I have some food. I'd be happy to share if…"

"No, we have plenty," I said.

"Calvin!" Hannah shouted with almost a whine. "Don't be telling her what we got."

Diana chuckled. "Smart kid. Can I travel with you?"

"Sure."

'No!" Hannah yelled. "No."

"Hold on," I told Diana then walked into the dugout. I lowered my voice. "Hannah, what's going on?"

"Nothin'. I don't want her coming. I don't trust her."

"Do you know her?" I asked. "You can tell me."

"No, I don't know her. I'd tell you if I did. We don't know her."

"We didn't know Mavis either. You were nice to her."

"Well, that's because she looked like my grandma. *She* doesn't." Hannah pointed at Diana. "Just because she's a woman don't mean she's not dangerous. I mean, where'd she come from Calvin? We ain't in plain view. Like she was wandering around looking for a ball field and said, 'Oh I'll stop there. Look people.' No. Don't trust her. She'll take our stuff. She'll try to kill Edward."

"She will not."

"The moment he makes a noise and attracts them things she will. Everyone wants to."

"Hannah, please. We'll watch her. Okay. I'll be diligent. If she is harmless, then we should let her join us. You and I both know there are some dangerous people out there."

"Fine." Hannah huffed, then whispered, "You remember the moment she does anything bad, she's gonna be a number one value meal."

"What are you talking about?" I asked.

Hannah raised her eyebrows. "You said we were a McDonald's menu. Remember?"

"My God, did you just suggest that?"

Hannah ignored me and went over to Edward. "I'm gonna get Edward ready. You get the horse and stuff."

I went back to Diana and put the backpack in the wagon. I explained we'd let Hannah adjust. Diana was fine with giving her space. I also explained that the horse still wasn't a hundred percent, and I was walking along side.

"Maybe for the last leg, we'll ride him in," I said.

"I don't mind walking," Diana replied.

"Hey, Hannah, I'm going to take the cart and wagon and head toward the road. "We'll eat in a few, okay?"

"Okay. Fine. I'm mixing his bottle. I'll be right there."

I grabbed the handle of the wagon and the horse's rein and started walking.

"She yours?" Diana asked.

"She is now. If that makes sense?"

"She's very protective."

"That's not a bad thing."

"Thank you for letting me join you. I've been on foot for weeks."

"No car?"

"Not since I ran out of gas outside of Cleveland," Diana said. "I promise to pull my weight. I am pretty..." she paused.

"What?"

"I'm pretty good with a gun. Stay back. I'll take care of this one." She pulled a revolver from the back of her pants, stepped ahead of me and lifted her arm.

It took a second to register what she was doing. Then it did. I let go of the rein and wagon and took a few steps forward.

Diana was aiming her gun... at Leah.

"No!" I shouted. "Stop. No!"

"What?" Diana was surprised. "She's one of the infected."

"Don't shoot that one. Not her. She's harmless. She won't bite. Please."

Diana lowered her weapon.

Just as she did, Hannah brushed by me.

"Yep. Don't listen to me," Hannah said as she walked ahead. "Been with us all about three minutes and already she's trying to shoot your wife."

"Your wife?" Diana asked, confused.

"I'll... I'll explain as we move. It's complicated." I walked back and grabbed the rein and wagon, and started walking.

21

PIPER

September 8

Crossing the main interstate was our targeted milestone for the day. Once we reached there we'd be in a position to stop for the night and the next day we'd be close to, if not at, Sanctuary Sixteen.

Leah slipped in distance, she would catch up when we paused, then slip back again. Diana walked side by side with me as I led the cart with Hannah and Edward and some of the supplies. She kept her back to Leah. I didn't blame her, I had a hard time not looking at her. Leah had begun to swell. Her stomach was huge, her arms and legs were bloated as well.

"Honestly, I don't think she'll bite us," I said.

"People say that all the time about pit bulls."

"I guess they do."

Diana looked over her shoulder. "You know what the progression of her body will be right?"

I shook my head.

"Right now, her body is bloating, filling with gasses. Her skin will break down and seep. Most of the Vee go through all the decomposition stages, then sort of slow down. The skin kind of tightens around what remains. The insects give up at that point. Very odd process, unnatural. Some say it has to do with a portion of the brain working. If the body is moving, then the circulatory system is working, even a little."

"What did you do before all this?" I asked.

"I've ran into several people, they don't believe me. You probably won't either."

"Try me."

"I was a professor of mortuary science."

"You're right," Hannah said. "We don't believe you."

"Hannah," I scolded. "So you taught people to be funeral directors."

"Yep. I did. I was a coroner first in Buffalo. Then I went into teaching. Because of my degrees in psychology and biology.... I never could decide what I wanted to be..."

Hannah made a scoffing noise.

Dianna shook her head with a smile. "Anyhow, I got pulled in to work with the outbreak when it hit Cleveland. Actually, I didn't have a choice."

"They made you work on the outbreak?"

"I worked with the Viral Enhanced. Or Vee as everyone calls them. I studied their anatomical breakdown, how some differed from others. They thought they had a way to bring them back. About six months ago, early in the outbreak, they had what they thought was a cure, or antidote."

"Did they?"

She shook her head. "No. It was hopeful. My job was to observe, examine and report. The medical examiner and pathologist were needed medically elsewhere. This thing got big. Your wife... she was bit."

"No kidding," Hannah said sarcastically.

Diana continued. "If I were to guess, somewhere that wasn't a deadly bite. Like arm or leg. She lived for a couple days. Most docile Vee were bit in nonlethal areas and took days to die. Because of the time it took the infection to kill them, most like that seemed to retain some mental capacities. Our study was never complete, but I know the Vee."

"If you know the Vee,' Hannah said. "Then does she know him?"

"There is no scientific evidence to support that," Diana answered. "However, from observation it seems something is retained. We just don't know what. She may not know him, but there's an instinct to follow him. Eventually though..." Diana stopped walking. "You will have to take care of your situation. It isn't mentally healthy for you to keep it going."

"I know. I know. I just didn't expect it to go on this long. I guess I won't have a choice when I get to Sixteen."

"No you won't."

"You know!" Hannah hollered. "You all keep whispering and talking like that, Leah will get jealous and no amount of mice is gonna stop her from going nuts."

"Oh, quit that," I told her, then looked to Diana. "Can that happen?"

"I don't know that it ever—"

I held up my hand to silence her, then whispered. "Shh."

We had arrived near the interchange that would take us to the interstate. There we would head west for two miles then catch another back road.

However, something was wrong. I not only smelled it, I heard it. Once all talking stopped and the clonking of Mary's hooves were no longer heard, the shuffling and groaning cut through the silence.

Unmistakably, it was the sound of the dead.

"Vee," I said.

"Calvin," Hannah whispered. "That sounds like a million of them."

"It does sound like a lot," Diana said. "Where though?"

After telling them to stay put, I followed the sounds. I crept through the brush on the side of the highway but didn't need to make it far to see what was happening.

Hundreds of Vee swarmed the road. They moved about aimlessly, back and forth. It reminded me of a concert crowd, just mobbed there.

Diana's one word of, "Here" made my jump from my skin. I grabbed my chest as she handed me a pair of binoculars.

"Jesus, you scared me."

"Sorry. Take a look. It goes just a quarter mile both ways. Trucks got them blocked in."

I saw what she had described. I hated that I saw them closer, some of them wandered about while eating something bloody. "How does that happen?"

"Someone did this to block the exit, I guess."

I handed her the binoculars and turned.

"What are you doing?" she asked.

"I want to look at our map."

Still remaining quiet, I made my way over to the cart, holding my fingers to my lips as a sign of 'quiet' to Hannah.

I pulled out the map and spread it out.

Hannah, without a sound moved her lips to ask, "What's going on?"

I pointed to where we were and spoke in a whisper, "Vee. Lots."

"What do you mean?"

"Try to keep the baby quiet while I figure this out," I said. "The Vee are blocking I-64 for about a quarter mile. They're penned in by trucks."

Diana returned, peering at the map. "Can we go around?"

"We could. It would add a day's journey especially if we backtrack and try the exit here…" I pointed. "Take that road for a while. It's all the wrong direction. Getting on the main highway is a straight shot back to Old Sixty and that's where we need to be…"

"So get on the highway," Hannah said.

"Hannah, there are hundreds," I explained. "Right here is the only place."

"It's a trap. Someone wants you to go around for a reason."

I nodded. "A reason, yes. I think just to keep that side of the highway safe."

"No, Calvin, I have a bad feeling. If the Vee are there, the only way to get them is to lead them. So lead them out. And why are they there? You know Vee look for food, right. I highly doubt animals are such a plenty that the Vee don't need to move."

"What are you saying Hannah? Someone is feeding them?" I asked.

"Yep. I say we play pied piper. They don't move fast. Heck, I'll do it. I'll go make noise, have them follow me. Once it's clear you get across."

"No." I shook my head. "If anyone is doing that, it's me."

"This is ridiculous," Diana said. "Look we don't need to back-track." She showed me on the map. "We're on old sixty now, right? We need to be on old sixty to get to Sixteen."

"Yeah, yeah," I said. "But old sixty loops up, too many hills and winding roads. Getting on I-64 cuts that all out.

"Hear me out," Diana said. "We stay on old sixty. It crosses over I-64 right where we are." She ran her finger. "Take it two miles, use the 1145 down here to get on I-64. Really we don't lose anything."

"Wow, I didn't even see that."

"Yeah," Hannah said with disbelief and lifted the map. "How the heck did you see that little bitty road? Kinda impressive. I thought old people couldn't see."

I quickly folded the map. "Let's get going. We need to be quiet though. When we go on the overpass, we don't need them to hear us."

"Calvin," Hannah grabbed my hand. "I really think this is a bad idea."

"Hannah," I said passively. "Listen. We're just running perpendicular. It's fine. Looks like only a couple miles to this 1145, then we'll be where we need to be. Okay?"

Hannah reluctantly agreed and continued on.

The highway was on flat land and a road leading to the fairgrounds was our original plan. That would take us to the highway. That was tossed out the window. Diana actually had a good back up route.

Leah didn't follow us, she went directly to the highway. Maybe she sensed food there, or something.

Seeing the Vee blockade from the overpass gave me a whole different perspective. It was obviously done on purpose. Trucks and vehicles made a fence of a large area, keeping them tight in there. I wondered why anyone would do that.

Then again, the town of Grayson was on the map. It was a small town, maybe they were all alive, they wanted to keep safe. Or maybe the Vee in the blockade were their loved ones and like me, they couldn't let go.

I didn't know and I didn't care. I just wanted to get going. We were close, so close.

Once we crossed the overpass, there was a short section of Old Sixty that ran ridiculously close to the Vee bull pen on the highway. It was a short section and by the time we had the coverage of trees between us and the highway, we had passed the blockade.

I noticed that the horse was stronger. The next day I would try to use the cart to bring us all to Sanctuary Sixteen. If I timed it right, and we left early in the morning, stopping to give Mary breaks every couple hours, we'd be there by nightfall.

I looked at my watch, it was pushing five o'clock and the sun would set soon. I figured we would stop once we hit that 1145, which I learned by looking closer at the map, was Aden Road. It had an underpass which was a great place to stop for the night.

I guess it was about a mile before the underpass when I spotted the Value Store eighteen-wheeler. I slowed down my walk and was apprehensive about moving forward. Was it another Vee blockade? Then I spotted the man on top of the truck. He held a rifle, but didn't aim it. He lifted it in a wave and I continued walking.

"What is this, Calvin?" Hannah asked. "See, I told you it was a trap."

As soon as I neared the truck, I saw what it blocked. Simple one lane road, led to two houses and a small white church with a Norman Rockwell steeple.

A few tents were set up on the land. There was a pig in a small pen and chickens roamed freely about.

I was curious about the place, but I had learned my lesson about stopping in populated areas outside of Sanctuary Sixteen.

I returned the wave to the man and kept going, only to be stopped by another man who came from around the truck.

A strong built man in his fifties with salt and pepper hair blocked the road. He did so almost arrogantly.

I zipped up my jacket so he didn't see the Glock in the waist of my pants. "We're just passing through. We aren't stopping," I said. "We would have been on the highway but it's blocked."

"Yep," he said and smiled. "That was us. We blocked that so people wouldn't come here."

"Maybe you should have blocked the overpass then."

He chuckled. "Maybe, but we need that to get supplies and we can see if someone is coming over that. Trent." He held out his hand.

"Calvin." I shook it. I looked beyond him to his set up. There was something off about it. Some sort of animal, maybe a pig was roasting and not far from it was a long table where three women went through backpacks and stacked canned goods and other items

He snapped his finger in front of me. "You with me?"

"I was just looking at your camp. Sorry."

"Beautiful horse." His eyes shifted to our cart.

"Yeah, he is."

"You fixin' to set up house somewhere permanently around here? By looks of all the stuff."

"No, we're headed to Sixteen."

"You're close. It's gonna be dark soon, I see you have kids and a woman. You sure you don't want to stop here? We're safe."

"We have a baby and he makes far too much noise. For the safety of others, I keep him away. But thank you, though."

"Are you sure? We do have a barter fee, it isn't too steep. You can have a safe place to sleep, some of our meat in exchange for goods."

For some reason, I looked at Hannah as if for approval. She shook her head then I told Trent, "No, thank you, we're going to get going."

"Good luck to you," he said.

"Yeah, you as well." I tugged on Mary's reins and started walking. Trent stood there watching us.

"Why didn't you want to stay?" Diana asked. "I would have given up my stuff."

"It didn't feel right," I said.

"Really, Calvin, we should have stopped."

"If you want to so bad…" Hannah yelled. "Go on. Catch us in the morning."

I wanted to scold Hannah, but I didn't. Diana was probably immune already to Hannah's flying insults.

A little down the road from Trent's camp, the highway came into view again. Sure enough, there was Leah walking in the same direction as us, all by herself down the center of the highway.

<><><><><>

The underpass provided a great shelter and plenty of room. I lit a small fire for warmth, and placed a heavy rock over the rope to the horse. It was the best I could do, there was nothing to tie him to.

Hannah played with Edward, had a little to eat, fed him in the cart, then asked if she could sleep there instead of the road. I didn't think that would be a bad idea.

I said goodnight to them both, grabbed one of my warm beers and walked to the road. I used the excuse that I wanted to take a piss, but I was really looking for Leah.

I didn't see her, yet I did sense she wasn't far.

"All better?" Diana asked when I returned.

"Yes." I took another swing of my beer and stepped by the cart. I could see Edward's dark hair peeking out from the carrier. His little fingers grasped a lock of Hannah's hair. I smiled and untangled Hannah's hair, lifted the carrier and placed it in the basket. I knew he was fine with Hannah, but I wanted him near me. I carried the basket and put it up the level part of the hillside just where the underpass met the ground. I figured that would block sound should he start to cry.

"Did you always want to be a father?" Diana asked.

I sat down across the fire from Diana. "Not really. When he was born, I knew I had no other purpose. There was something very special about him. Plus, I had lost his mother."

Diana tilted her head. "Not really."

"Okay maybe not."

"You think she's gone now?"

"No. I don't feel it." I finished my beer. "How about you? Did you always want to be a mother?"

"Yes. I love being a mother."

"You didn't use past tense," I said.

"Because I believe they're alive. They're safe out there. I know it. I feel it."

"I hope you find them."

"Thank you."

She must have noticed my yawn. "Why don't I take first watch? You're tired and Edward will start making a fuss soon enough."

"Are you sure?"

"Positive. Get some sleep."

"Thank you. Wake me if you need anything." I walked back to the cart, grabbed a sleeping bag and carried it up to lie down next to Edward. It didn't take long to fall asleep. That beer probably helped.

I dreamt too. A weird dream. I was at an amusement park set up at the Value Store parking lot. Hannah laughed and giggled then she got on the ride that swung her around. Each time I watched her pass she would call my name with her arms in the air.

I kept looking at her and the strong man, raising that hammer and landed it on the surface trying to ring the bell, but he kept missing and the hammer made a 'crack' sound.

"Calvin," Hannah called.

She whizzed by me.

Crack.

"Calvin, help me."

When the swinging ride circled again, she was hanging on.

Crack.

"Calvin!"

Hannah screamed.

That was when I realized, she really was calling my name, and the crack of the strong man was a gunshot.

Just as I sprang awake, I heard another scream. That one was pain and it was not coming from Hannah.

Panicking, I slid down the hill as the cart moved from the underpass.

Diana cried out, her screams curdled as she hung on to the cart with Leah locked to her arm.

I ran after them, a man was driving the cart, pushing the horse to move. He picked up speed and Diana dropped off. Hannah screamed my name, reaching out.

The man driving reached back and hit her, knocking her down into the cart.

My heart raced, Leah had lunged onto Diana. Diana also reached out.

"Help," she said. It didn't look as if she were looking at me.

Leah released her and stepped away. I hurried to Diana.

"I'm sorry she did this," I said. "I have to get Hannah."

She coughed and choked, blood poured from her arm and chest. She lifted her head and once again looked beyond me.

"Kill him," she coughed out the words.

"What?"

I turned and before I could do anything, I saw a figure and something struck down at me.

Everything went black.

I regained consciousness for a moment, only to realize I was moving in some sort of vehicle. I made the mistake of calling out Hannah's name and it was lights out again, until I felt my back hit on the cold hard ground.

I opened my eyes.

I didn't need to see very well to know what was happening and where I was. I was the proverbial feed for the watch dogs. I was on that highway, on my back surrounded by Vee.

22

FEAST

My first thought was, *This is how it ends.*

Right there, on the dark highway alone, I would be torn to shreds.

This was how it would end.

I never worried about the Vee as much as I should have, mainly because I never thought they'd get me. Vee moved slow, I moved faster.

Yet... this was how it would end.

My eyes adjusted pretty quickly. The sky was clear, the moon was bright and I would see it all unfold. Ripped to shreds, eaten while I would still comprehend what was happening. I wasn't terrified for myself. I was terrified for Hannah. What would they do to her? And Edward, did they take him? Kill him?

I didn't even know.

I was useless and helpless. My body was still healing from the previous attack, I wasn't even sure I could move. A lightning speed of thoughts went through my mind. A part of me was glad that it was over, yet, I knew if my child had been spared and Hannah not killed, they would face a horrendous world. One where the Vee weren't the enemy, they were the obstacle. Man took the opportunity to be the vilest of creatures. Even if mankind survived and outlived the Vee, humanity was dead.

I was proof of this by lying there as the next Vee meal.

Hannah was right. It was trap; a twelve-year-old girl saw it and I didn't. The blockade of Vee forced us to move forward and we walked right into the trap.

I heard her voice in my mind.

"You know Vee look for food, right. I highly doubt animals are such a plenty that the Vee don't need to move."

"What are you saying Hannah? Someone is feeding them?"

"Yep."

To me, she was being absurd that someone was feeding them to keep them in one place. Yet, there I was the next meal. Who were these people as to be so cruel to do that to someone? Were my belongings worth more than my life?

Apparently so.

It stunk. Rotting flesh mixed with a sour odor. It was thick and I was in the middle of it.

About six of them encircled me. Part of me wanted one of them to be Leah. If any Vee killed me, I'd rather it be her. Leah had her fill; she took a good bite out of Diana.

I knew it was a matter of seconds before rest came. Then I felt it, the gun in the waist of my pants. They hadn't taken it. They didn't even know I had it.

I reached for it, shifted the chamber and with a trembling hand put it to my head. I would pull the trigger before they took their first bite.

The moment the first hand reached down and touched me, I didn't want to die. I thought about shooting them, but I didn't know how many rounds I had in the gun and I wasn't all that good of a shot.

This was how it ends... no. Not yet.

Edward was possibly unharmed or unnoticed. For all I knew he was in that basket screaming for help.

And Hannah... I promised her I would watch her, take care of her.

If I were going to die, then I would go down fighting.

I swatted away the first hand and kicked another Vee out of my way, enabling myself to roll to my knees and then stand. I thought again about shooting, but if I were going to try to get Hannah, then I couldn't let them hear the shots.

My best way out was to fight and run.

They came for me. Hands grabbing my clothing. I spun and fought, trying not to get bitten or scratched. I knew I had speed and they didn't. I was like a football player, charging my way through.

I broke free to a clearing only to trip over something. My hands smeared in the thick substance as I tried to stand up and my eyes caught the portion of the arm.

That was what they did. They didn't barter a safe night. They convinced people to stay, knocked them out cold, took them to the Vee pen and kept their belongings.

I wasn't out cold and I vowed I would not be one of their statistics. After making it to my feet, I dodged another. I believed it was only by the grace of God that I was able to fight my way out. By way of only a moonlit night, I pushed, shoved, kicked and focused to get off that highway. I aimed for the Value Store tractor trailer; that was my goal to get to.

Finally, I did. There was an opening between that truck and another, and once I slipped through, I stopped to catch my breath. I had about a mile and a half good run to get to Trent's place, because surely, that was who took Hannah.

I had to come up with a plan and do so quickly. I was the meal that was getting away and the Vee were pursuing me. They never slipped through the openings between the trucks because they were given incentive to stay.

Now they had incentive to leave.

They were going to make it difficult. Fending off the Vee while trying to figure out a way to get Hannah and get the people that took her.

Then, once more, I heard the voice in my head of that wise twelve-year-old girl.

"The only way to get them is to lead them. So lead them out."

With that thought, her words, and the Vee right before me, the lightbulb went on and I smiled.

23

PSALMS

It was perfect. A mere fifty feet of level area separated the highway from the road I needed to take to get to Trent's. Funny how twelve hours earlier I was worried that the Vee would spot us, now I wanted them to.

I moved slowly. Occasionally darting close to them to catch my scent, then backing up enough for them to see and follow me. The slow pace allowed me to gain my focus, not get winded and figure out what I needed to do.

One thing that worried me was the guard on top of the truck. Would he be able to see the Vee heading his way, would he even look? I know they mentioned seeing people cross the overpass... was the road out of their range of sight?

In case it wasn't, I stayed near the side of the road.

My plan was to get close enough to that truck without being spotted, then make my way quickly into their camp, while bringing the Vee near enough to catch the scent of everyone there.

I didn't worry or feel guilty about the Vee attacking them. Surely, they'd be able to fight them off. I could and they had weapons.

I just wanted Hannah back and hopefully, they had Edward. I didn't even want to process the idea that they murdered him in that basket back at the underpass.

Moving at a snail's pace, I made it just to the edge of the truck, certain, he didn't spot me. He did however, I assumed, spot the mob of Vee.

He whistled once and called out, "We have trouble."

He wasn't looking my way and I raced around the front of the truck to the single lane road into their camp.

Sure enough there was my horse, still attached to the cart. Our belongings, including the red wagon were sprawled out everywhere and Trent along with two others were picking through them.

"What do you see?" Trent, standing above my wagon, asked the man on the truck.

I pulled the Glock and raced his way.

"Hard to count, we have a lot of them headed this way."

Trent was preoccupied exchanging words with the man on the truck so I took that as my opening.

The moment he moved to walk toward the truck, I aimed the gun.

"Where is she?!" I blasted, arm held out.

He seemed annoyed and waved a couple of his men to go to the truck.

"Well take a look at the second person ever to get out of the pit. Congrats for having bigger balls than I gave you credit. Now if you don't mind…"

"I do mind. Where is she?"

"I don't have time for this shit!" he yelled.

"Neither do I! Where is she?"

"Calvin!" Hannah raced down the hillside. Even at a distance I could see her bruised and bloody face. As soon as she got near, Trent reached out, and with a single swat sent her flying back.

"You son of a bitch!"

"What are you gonna do, shoot me?" he asked.

"Give me the girl and I'll be on my way."

"She's better off here, you know it."

"Oh, yeah she looks it. Come on Hannah."

"She got out of control. She is still better off here!" Trent yelled. "Diana told me about your dead tag along. You think that's better for her?"

"Mr. Trent!" someone hollered. "They're in."

A scream somewhere in camp rang out.

Hannah again tried to get to me and when Trent reached for her again, I fired.

The bullet didn't hit him. It hit the ground. He did step back, though.

"Let her go!" I shouted and fired and again. I missed.

"What the fuck is wrong with you? You're a joke," Trent said.

I fired again.

Trent laughed. "You gonna waste your bullets on me, at least try not to miss those things."

Another shot. Another miss. My finger stayed on the trigger. I could hear the pandemonium and gun fire, the others were too preoccupied to worry about me.

"I'd worry," Trent continued to taunt and laugh. "But damn, I'm ten feet from you. You couldn't hit the side of a barn if you—"

He was immediately silenced when I finally landed a shot. This one was spot on and dead center of his forehead.

I raced to Hannah, and helped her up. "Let me get you out of here and we'll take care of you. Where's Edward?"

"He's not here."

A sickening feeling hit me about my son, but I had to get out of there. It was the perfect opportunity. The whole camp was focused on the Vee attack. "Let's go." I grabbed her hand and we ran to the cart.

"What about our stuff?"

I helped her in the cart. "We don't need it." I hurried and untied the horse.

"Calvin, we do. We need food. We need our stuff…"

"Go. Go to the underpass, take it slow. Go, I'll catch up." I placed the Glock on her lap, handed Hannah the reins, gave Mary a swift pat to her rear and the horse trotted off.

In a low run, I made it to the pile where our stuff had been thrown. There was no way I would grab it all, but I moved fast, really fast. I just needed enough to get us through for two days. Her Barbie backpack and another backpack were open but not emptied. I zipped up her Barbie pack, then shoved what I could into the other backpack. I threw that in and a few other things into the wagon, and as I grabbed for more items, I felt the hand on my back and smelled the scent of Vee.

Quickly, I lifted that Barbie pack and while coming to a stand, swung out full speed, nailing the Vee and sending him off his balance.

I tossed the Barbie pack on my shoulder, lifted the jug of water, tossed that in the wagon, grabbed the handle and moved toward the road.

That wagon was a lot lighter than it had ever been and I pulled it with ease, hoping to not lose anything out of it. When I hit the end of the dirt road, I was cautious to look and make sure there were no Vee. There weren't.

I took one more look back.

Some Vee were victorious in getting their victims, but for the most part, the Trent Camp was fighting and wouldn't be wiped out.

They'd be looking for us and we couldn't waste any time.

There was no way we could stop. By first light, they'd be after us.

I caught up to Hannah and the cart after a mile. I called out when I was close enough and she stopped.

I tossed everything in the back of the cart, then walked to the horse and spoke in his ear. "I'm sorry to put this strain on you. You'll rest shortly, okay?" I ran my hand down his mane and climbed to the bench driver's seat. I stared at Hannah with a sympathetic look, snapped the reins and we moved down the road. It was a short distance to the underpass where we'd stopped previously for the night.

My heart was filled with fear over what I would find. It pounded louder in my ears every few feet. I was certain that I would see Leah on the ground and was surprised when I only saw Diana.

She stood in the middle of the road right before the underpass.

"She one of them?" Hannah asked.

"Yeah, it appears so." I moved closer.

"Stop."

I pulled the reins to bring us to a stop.

Hannah stood and extended the gun.

"Let me," I said.

"No offense, Calvin, but we can't have you wasting all our ammo hoping for a lucky shot."

"You think you can hit her in the dark like…"

She fired the weapon and Diana fell back.

"Okay then."

Hannah handed me the gun, then stopped me from moving. She laid her hand on mine. "Calvin, what do you think we'll find with Edward?"

"I don't know. We'll find out in a minute."

The horse began to walk and in the few moments, every horrible scenario imaginable ran through my mind. Diana had gotten him or even Leah. Worse, whoever knocked me out just curb stomped Edward. Each thought made my heart hurt.

Then that ended with a simple whimper. It cut through the night loudly and I gasped out in relief.

Hannah nearly shrieked with joy.

I brought the cart to a stop, jumped out and ran. Sure enough the basket was still nestled up on top of the grade against the overpass, right where I put him.

They never touched him.

The basket hadn't been moved.

I lifted him out and hugged him close to my chest with such an enormous amount of gratitude. I was fortunate and blessed. "You are one tough kid," I said to him. "One really special tough boy."

It seemed every stop was another lesson, and I was learning from them. Once I finished holding Edward, I brought him to the cart and handed him to Hannah. I knew we had to move, but I had to take care of Hannah first.

Using the jug of water, I took a shirt and brought it to Hannah. I climbed up on the bench and made her face me.

"I'm fine."

"No, you're not." I wiped her bloody mouth and nose. Her cheek was swollen and brush burned. "I'm sorry this happened to you. I am so sorry."

She clutched my hand and for the first time, I watched a tear roll down her check. She released a single sob and her forehead fell to my hand and I brought her into my chest, holding her.

"Calvin," she peeped out.

"Yeah,"

"You told Mama Mavis you ain't no hero. Never say that again. You're the bravest man I know. You're a hero to me, okay?"

"Okay." I kissed the top of her head.

"Promise you won't leave me, Calvin. Promise me you'll stay with me."

"I promise I won't leave you."

We had our moment, now it was time to move on. We had to. Hannah held Edward, and with one arm holding her to me, I used the other to control the cart and we left the underpass slowly, but we left it alive and all together.

24

September 9

It started to rain just before the sun came up and it was a blessing more than a curse. There were no signs of the Trent camp people following us. I couldn't count on that always being that way. I just needed to get us to Sixteen before they got us.

There was a chance they wouldn't come. Maybe they suffered so much of their own losses, we were an afterthought. I certainly hoped so.

I suspected they'd expect us to take the interstate. Instead, with only a tiny lighter size flashlight, I was able to see that Aden Road, would take us to another back road and eventually to Old Highway 60. Only four miles extra out of the way. I felt it was a safe route for us.

That journey on those roads took hours, Mary wasn't moving very fast and I didn't want to push her. The tree lined road gave us little protection from the rain and fallen leaves made the road slick. The wheels of the cart kept sliding every once in a while.

By the time we made it to an interchange town called Counts Crossroads, we had enough of a head start to stop. It was on my original itinerary and I was bit leery of stopping, but we had to. Just a couple hours, just enough to rest, and then we'd push forward. I had no plans to stop for the night, not anymore. Even if the sun went down, we'd forge ahead. It was ten in the morning, we'd be there soon enough.

We were so close. Twenty-one miles. I knew from experience it wasn't good to push a horse more than fifteen miles on concrete, but knowing that Jason had made the trip in five days, told me he pushed it to the limits.

It was the most cautious I had ever felt on the journey, looking out, peering around. There were no Vee that I could see and there were no people. There was a vast amount of abandoned cars, doors left open, some off to the side of the road. From Counts Crossroads to Sanctuary Sixteen it was possibly a one day walk for someone with stamina. Hell, people in the military walked that much a lot.

Our supplies were drenched, and the three places in town that had supplies were wiped clean, I should have expected as much.

It was cold and I found the ideal place to stop.

Just outside of town, part of the high school system was a career and technical institute. I remember when I was in high school, even though I excelled in math, I was a poor student, hated school and did afternoon classes at one of those tech schools.

I had hoped they had a mechanic course, which would mean a garage. It looked like it might. A small administrative-style building with a huge warehouse structure attached to the back. After following the driveway, I found the triple wide sliding garage door.

It was locked.

I checked out the exterior of the grounds, saw no Vee, but the front doors were glass. I left the cart behind the building.

"I'll be back," I told Hannah.

She nodded. She looked tired as if she didn't feel well. I knew she didn't.

I looked around the grounds on my way to the front and found a large stone. I kept thinking how did anyone miss this place? How was it untouched? Maybe people were so focused on the obvious supply places, they didn't think of a technical school, or they realized how close they were to Sanctuary and didn't care.

An easy throw of the rock shattered the glass and I kicked it clean with my foot. The lobby was dusty and smelled of dust, no one had been in the building a while and the air was stale.

After checking out the fire exit map on the wall, I walked my way through the small classroom building, checking every room to make sure it was safe. I arrived to where the garage would be. It wasn't mechanical, it was carpentry.

The smell of wood filled the air, only a small window let in a little light. Sheets of plywood were stacked up against the wall and I opened the huge garage door.

The area was large and I led the horse and cart inside and closed the door.

We were hidden and safe. It was more than I could ask for.

<><><><>

The technical school was a gold mine. The carpentry area had flashlights and battery operated lanterns. The first thing I did was secure our safety. I grabbed the plywood and I sealed up the front of the building and the broken window. I was confident no one would know we were in there and the building was far enough away that no one would hear Edward.

By the time I finished securing the front and all the doors, nearly two hours had passed.

Hannah followed me around even after I advised her not to.

"I don't understand, Calvin, you said we were only staying a couple hours."

"I think we'll stay a little longer. You need to rest. I want to clean those bruises, bandage you and have you lay down on a real bed."

She snickered. "Calvin, how you gonna do all that?"

"This way." I took her arm and led her to the back. "Here. The medical teaching room."

She peeked inside and smiled when she saw the examining bed. "There are people in them."

"They're mannequins."

"I knew that." She looked at me. "Okay. I'm gonna lay down. Wake me if you need me to feed Edward. I mean, I just did, so he should be good until we go."

"I appreciate that. Now, let me bandage you up then you sleep. When you feel ready to go, we'll go."

I found what I needed in that teaching hall. I cleaned her bruises, put on ointment, even made her take some ibuprofen. It didn't take long for her to fall asleep and I made the most of my time.

I went through our supplies to determine what was salvageable and what was not, then I hit the vending machines and took what I could.

I was most productive in the garage. In fact, I was inventive. Using two by fours, I made four posts around the cart and used a tarp I found to create a cover. Then after finding two sheets of tin in the metal shop, I rigged two of the spotlights to the front posts on the cart to create my own version of headlights. I did the best I could to shield the lights with the tin, to protect from the rain, but I didn't see that lasting long.

The final leg of the trip was ahead of us and I just wanted to get there safely, rain or shine, light or dark.

25

SANCTUARY

Hannah slept for three hours straight. When she woke up she looked better and felt better. She started rambling and I knew she was getting back to her old self. I was glad.

I asked her if she wanted to stay, but she was insistent that we leave. So we packed up and would be on the road two hours before sundown. To my surprise and a little relief, Leah was at the bottom of the driveway.

"She must have a wife GPS on your rear end," Hannah said. "I can't believe she found us."

"It's weird."

"Yeah, but I saw her back when we left the underpass and then again when you stopped to pee. She was closing in."

"Why didn't you say anything?" I asked.

"Because you didn't mention her and I thought maybe you were mad that she ate a person."

"No, I'm not mad."

We started moving and Leah tagged behind. There was a steady slight drizzle, but the tarp kept us dry.

"We should have stayed at the school," I said. "Really. We were safe."

"They were coming, Calvin. I don't think they'd go past that town, but they were coming there."

"Why do you say that?" I asked.

"Because you told that woman everything."

I nodded in agreement. "True."

"I told you not to trust her, but there you went trusting her, and telling her your inner most secrets."

"Oh, please, I did not."

"You did. Didn't I tell you Leah was gonna get jealous? Ate her right up. Speaking of Leah…" Hannah looked behind us. "Whatcha gonna do about her? She can't come into Sanctuary with us."

"I know."

"She'll follow us there. She'll get there after us and they'll shoot her."

"I know."

"Think you should do it first?"

"Hannah, I don't know if I can. I mean… I know what she is."

"It'll hurt your feelings if someone else does it. I know. I know how I felt when Pastor Jim killed my Dad."

"You saw it though, maybe it won't hurt if I don't."

"Maybe."

As I thought it over, we lost Leah again. She trailed behind unable to keep up. She was back there and I knew it.

After it turned dark, we stopped for an hour. Edward was out of control, even Hannah taking him aside, walking him and feeding him didn't help.

I felt inside of me he was sick. He had caught pneumonia or something. He didn't sound right. After all he had been through I was surprised that he was still moving. His crying was a calling card for Leah, a way to find us in the night, and she did.

I gave the choice to Hannah if she wanted to stay put or move forward. We had less than ten miles to go and Hannah wanted to forge ahead. She managed to calm him down with the pacifier.

After getting her in the cart, I stood by the side, Edward strapped to my chest and looked at Leah.

"This is goodbye you know," I told her. "I know you don't understand me, but we'll lose you before we get there. I just needed to say goodbye."

Of course, Leah tilted her head. She stared back, the skin on her face was drawing in giving her an anorexic appearance. I looked once more then got in the cart and drove.

The homemade headlights worked but we had to slow down the pace. Then just as we saw a sign for Morehead, KY that we had three miles remaining, a massive storm blew in. I felt it coming earlier. The wind picked up and phantom lightning flashed in the sky without the sound of thunder.

Then it hit. The rain blew sideways and the tarp sailed off. Edward squirmed in the carrier and I tried my hardest to keep that covered.

There was absolutely nowhere to stop. Those last couple miles seemed like hundreds. The wind and rain hit us so hard, we were moving against a huge wet current. We inched our way down the road

The first spotlight went out, then the next.

"I have to stop!" I shouted, the only way Hannah could hear me.

"No! Keep going."

"It's not safe. It's too wet for the baby."

"He's fine. You have him covered. We're so close, Calvin we're…"
She stopped.

I pulled the reins, stopping the horse. The sight took my breath away and I finished her sentence. "Here."

Not far ahead of us, the brightness cut through the black of the night. Huge amounts of light lit up the horizon. It was Sanctuary. That was the only thing it could be.

A snap of the reins and we had a guiding light. Then I saw what looked like spotlights ahead. Like the kind you see at night on road construction sites. They were brighter the closer we moved. It clearly was a roadblock. Then we started seeing Vee. More Vee than I had seen the entire day. They moved about on the side of the road, as we approached, some even reached for the cart.

I moved faster, the rain beating against my face.

"Calvin, you don't think they're overrun, do you?"

"We'll find out."

We made our approach and a feeling of awe took over me when I saw the entrance ahead. Two giant spotlights lit up the area. A large tunnel on the road was created from a fence with a barbed wire arched ceiling.

A light swung on us, nearly blinding me, then it moved.

Two armed guards stood by the barricade and one waved us in.

The rain pelted down and I swiped the water from my eyes as I stopped the cart.

A soldier wearing rain gear approached. "I thought you were a man I knew named Jason," he spoke loudly over the noise of the rain.

"Jason passed away," I told him. 'He had a heart attack."

"Ah man. That's sad. He was a good guy."

"Is this Sanctuary Sixteen?" I asked.

"It is. Sorry I didn't shoot those things out there. We're not allowed. Gun fire attracts at night."

"I understand," I said. "We made it. We just want in."

"Absolutely. She okay?" he asked, shining his flashlight on Hannah's face.

"Yes. We ran into trouble."

The soldier then hit me with the beam of the light. "We'll check you inside for bites." Again he moved his light on Hannah. "Is her arm bandaged?"

I looked over. Her arm was outside of the blanket. The bandage was wet and stained.

"It's not a bite or scratch. She was injured. It opened back up when she was attacked. They can see inside!"

"Not hiding anyone in the back, are you?" He moved the light. "Just the two of you?"

"Three!" I said. "Me, her, and the baby. He's a newborn." I pointed down and adjusted the carrier.

He moved his flashlight to the carrier. "Sir, there are no…" He stopped when the light hit Edward's face as he sucked on the pacifier. The soldier's eyes went from Edward to me. "Sir…" his voice softened. "You cannot come in here with that."

"What are you talking about?" I asked. "He's a baby."

"Calvin," Hannah reached out and touched my arm. "Let's just go. We'll go back to Mama Mavis."

"No, we're here." I turned to the soldier. "Are babies not allowed?"

"Babies would be allowed. We don't allow Formers. The dead can't get in, no matter what shape or form they are. I'm sorry. You can't bring…"

"Calvin, let's go," Hannah pleaded.

"What do you mean dead?" I asked. "He's just a baby."

"There are no babies, sir! There hasn't been a baby born uninfected in six months."

"But…"

Then my mind slipped back and I heard Mr. Mills that day I met him. "*Son, there shouldn't be a baby in this godforsaken world, you know that.*"

235

"Even to healthy mothers," the soldier said. "They're coming out that way."

"No." I shook my head. The soldier was wrong. He had to be mistaken.

"Man, I heard that thing crying all night." Was what the man in Marshal said when he tried to rob me.

Then when Trent told me, *"Diana told me about your dead tag along,"* surely, he was talking about Leah. Or was he?

No, was I blinded? Was I missing it?

"Sir, you can come in. But you can't bring that in here."

"Calvin," Hannah said my name with a whimper. "We don't need to stay. You love Edward."

"Sir, move it to the side and go through or—"

"He don't know!" Hannah shouted. "He doesn't see. Leave him be a second!"

"What do you mean I don't know?" I asked. "See what? Hannah, you have been…" Every ounce of breath left me. She calmed him down… always. She made Edward quiet.

"I… fed him for you."

"Boy, I have to tell you, Hannah, you have the magic touch with him."

"I know what I'm doing. Mom said it takes patience to feed a baby right and know what it wants."

I finally finished my own sentence, "…feeding him." My eyes shifted to her bloody bandage and then to Edward. The pacifier dropped from his mouth; it was blood stained as was his mouth.

"He didn't touch the cut," Hannah cried. "I just dripped some in his bottle. His pacifier…"

"No." The rain beat down, the lightning flashed and in that instance the fog was lifted. He hadn't turned into it, he hadn't died on the trip. Edward like every other baby, was born a Vee.

His eyes shifted about, they were gray and lifeless. His skin was leathery and split in some places. His hand had rotted and several of his fingers were gone. "No. No." I shook my head. "How… why didn't I know?"

"You weren't ready to know," Hannah said. "You lost your wife, you didn't want to know. He's all you had."

A deep ache filled my chest, I wanted to scream, to cry out, but all that emerged was a sob. I would have broken down had another soldier not approached.

"What's going on?" the second soldier asked.

"We have a bit of a problem."

The second that other soldier saw Edward he pulled out his pistol.

"No!" I shouted. "No! I'll take him away. No." I stepped from the cart, my feet splashed in the puddle when I touched the road.

"Calvin, where are you going?" Hannah shouted.

I began to sob as I cradled Edward in my arms and headed away from Sanctuary. My heart was broken. I had carried him, cared for him and worried about Edward the entire journey. I loved and needed him so badly. I was blinded by what he truly was.

"Calvin, you can't leave me!" Hannah yelled. "You promised! You promised me!"

Her voice faded as I moved further down the road, the rain was loud as it fell around me drowning out the sound of everything. I knew where I was going and what I had to do. I knew she had to be there.

She was.

Leah stood in the middle of the road. Everything was clear. I wondered why she followed me so fervently. Maybe I was wrong, or still delusional, but it wasn't me that she was following.

I moved close to Leah and pressed my lips to Edward's head. "Goodbye, I love you, little one." Then I extended the baby to Leah.

"Take him," I said. "Take the baby."

I didn't know what she would do, she stared at me for the longest time, hesitating before she grabbed Edward and brought the baby to her chest.

When she did that, I knew it was time to leave. A searing pain radiated through my chest, it hurt to breathe and I took a few steps back.

Leah turned, walked away and for the first time in the journey, she didn't follow me. She just kept going.

It was my cue to do the same. I said a final goodbye to my wife and I knew it was the last time I would see her. I bid farewell to my son, as well, but it wasn't the last time I would be a father. Another child needed me.

I would be there for her and I headed back to Sanctuary Sixteen.

26

EXPIRE

October 10

Mama Mavis greeted us with open arms. In fact. She ran down the road to greet us and told us she was thrilled the second she saw it was us.

As Hannah predicted, she was sad about Jason. However, she figured something had happened to him when he never returned.

Her husband George had expired a week earlier.

In fact, there was a lot of expiring.

The night we had arrived at Sanctuary Sixteen, both Hannah and I were more physically and emotionally exhausted than we realized.

I knew the second we stepped in there that we weren't staying. Like we were told, we had to surrender our belongings. Because everyone knew Jason, and I vocalized that our stay was temporary, they didn't claim our horse and cart. I was told it would be ours to have.

We couldn't leave though, until one week after the last city had been purged.

The college town of Morehead was nothing but a massive tent city. They crammed people together, rows and rows of cots in each tent. Not a spot of grass could be seen.

Dogs and cats were not permitted and food was distributed to tents once a week. Rations were meager and they tossed in a few items I suspected came from the belongings they seized from arrivals.

I was scared that Hannah was infected with the virus. That somehow she had caught it from Edward. It wasn't the case. Because she continuously opened her wound to give him blood, her cut just didn't heal.

Both she and I spent the first week in a medical tent. I was on some sort of watch because they weren't certain of my mental state. I wasn't either. I took 'denial' to the extreme.

After that, we were given quarters where we shared a tent with an eighty-year-old couple. They were nice enough, both had lost everyone to the virus. The woman, Ernesta, prepared all our meals from our rations. She wouldn't let me help at all.

Staying with her, reminded us of Mavis and we couldn't wait to return.

While there I told Hannah about my boss Martin and how he had a survival place in Montana. She said it was a sign that his first name was Mavis' last name, and that maybe we should go to Montana.

I simply told her, "Maybe."

A rumor started around the camp that the fire bombings of the cities were a waste, that the Vee infected from the waves were expiring. That the 'dead' really only walked for a month.

Many disputed those rumors, claiming that the older Vee were gone but the virus wasn't. They'd always be there and be a threat.

The old way of life was gone. It was a new world.

One thing was certain, I was healed physically and emotionally.

I was a new person, my family was Hannah now. However, not a day went by when I didn't think of Leah or Edward.

By the time we were able to leave Sanctuary, several of the soldiers confirmed the rumors of the expiring Vee and new Vee emerging, though not as many as in the beginning. People stayed behind the fences, needing the provisions and protection that Sanctuary offered. Sanctuary was their new home.

I believe many more would have left, but there was no way to know truly what was going on in the world, except to go see.

As the horse-drawn cart brought us down Old Sixty, I admittedly looked. I kept looking to see if I saw Leah or Edward, or even their remains. Alas, they were gone.

I prayed they expired together, that Leah simply sat down with Edward in her arms and finally passed from this life, instead of being gunned down like animals.

We did see the bodies of many expired. I wondered if they would be cleaned up one day or just left to turn to dust. My guess was it would be the latter.

We made it to Mama Mavis' place in three days after leaving Sanctuary. I never saw one person so happy to see me. It was the right decision to go back there.

Perhaps one day, for Hannah's sake, she and I would brave another road trip, maybe to Montana or just to see the world and meet other people. We would wait though, it was still too dangerous. People made it dangerous and it would be up to people to make it better again.

Life as we knew it was gone. No television, radio or internet. There were no new books to read, or songs to hear. Pockets of society thrived while others deteriorated. News traveled by word of mouth, and it was few and far between when we saw another person.

One day the Vee would disappear. Each generation would grow smaller, and eventually there would be no more.

Until the world was truly purged of the monsters, both living and dead, Hannah and I would stay put at that little farm on the border of West Virginia and Kentucky. We were given a chance not just to survive in a dying world, but to be alive.

For the time being, we'd take it day by day, grieving our losses, grateful for the chance at life, and hopeful that somehow, someway, I'd live long enough to see the better world I knew was ahead for us all.